I0589863

This anthology has been published by FAWNW (Fellowship of Australian Writers North West, a branch of the Fellowship of Australian Writers).

The branch has been operating for over fifty years and its members are spread widely along the North West Coast of Tasmania and occasionally further afield.

Meetings are held monthly. Visitors are always welcome.

Contact: fawtas@y7mail.com for details.

Published by:
FAWNW
c/o Allan Jamieson
P.O. Box 608
Burnie
Tasmania
Australia 7320

Roads in a Yellow Wood

Collated: Allan Jamieson
Editors: Ant Dry and Dawn Meredith

The 2019 anthology of FAWNW
(Federation of Australian Writers – North West branch)

The title, *Roads in a Yellow Wood*, alludes to Robert Frost's 1916 poem *The Road Not Taken*: 'Two roads diverged in a yellow wood, and sorry I could not travel both…'

Roads in a Yellow Wood

Table of Contents
(S) = short story; (P) = poem

A HOLIDAY FROM HELL
Ant Dry

It was just another day in hell. Lucifer sat and looked at the throngs queuing to see him. As far as he could see they stood, in long lines all downcast, eyes to the floor, quaking in fear.

For millennia, he had enjoyed the sight and had happily played out the part handed to him by God. He had cheerfully thrown millions into the fiery furnaces and watched them as they vaporised. He had enjoyed watching as crocodiles sprang to do his bidding and had devoured sinners with gusto. He had invented drawing and quartering and had personally supervised zillions to be flayed alive. All great fun and all in a day's work.

Somehow today though, he wasn't in the mood.

Mrs Lucifer had noticed it at breakfast.

"What's eating you?" she'd asked, "Brimstone off this morning? We ran out of milk so it may be a bit tart for you."

It hadn't been the brimstone though, but he couldn't put his finger on it.

"Excuse me Sir?" It was Paddington, one of his better ghouls

"Sorry Paddington, what's the problem?"

"This man Jones Sir."

"Ah, yes, Jones – UUMM – What was it all about then?"

Paddington looked quizzically at his master.

"He's a murderer, Sir. What's it to be? Drawing and quartering or flaying alive?"

Normally Lucifer would have entered into the fray and the discussion would rage for hours as Jones (or whoever) stood and shivered miserably.

"Your name Jones?" Lucifer addressed the man.

There was a shocked and deathly silence in the hall. Lucifer never spoke directly to any of the sinners or at least he hadn't in the last 10 874 years. There had been a time back then, and everyone had forgotten the details, but no one had forgotten that it had happened. It had been a shock then and had been the first time ever. The man addressed began to blubber. Paddington slapped him across the back of the head.

"Answer his worship you fool," he muttered

"Yes Sire. I murdered my wife and I'm very sorry Sire. Please don't flay me alive."

"Why ever not? Isn't that what you want? I thought that was what all murderers wanted."

"No Sire, please no."

"Oh alright then, just this once. Paddington, draw and quarter him then, if that's what he wants. Bugger this for a joke; I'm going to the pub." And he stood up and walked out.

The Pub was full as usual. All the local ghouls and goblins were there, fighting and trying to gouge each other's eyes out. Two bloodied corpses lay on the floor in front of the counter.

"A pint of your best please Charlie" Lucifer called out

"We have a new vintage on line, Sir, MH370, it's very fresh."

"The blood ran thickly from the tap.

"Hmm. Looks good."

As he sat there, feeling a bit miserable, sipping on his blood beer, Lucifer wondered what the problem was.

As he drained his tankard, it came to him. In a blinding flash, he realised what the problem was. He was sick of it. He had worked solidly for 20,000 years and he was sick of it. He needed a holiday.

A holiday from hell.

SYLVANIA
Dawn Meredith

"Good morning." I close my office door behind her, smile and offer the woman my hand. "I'm Donna."

She regards me with cold eyes. A middle-aged woman, with greying hair and an early stoop, she is dressed plainly in a cotton dress. Muttering a reply she walks past me, straight past the comfortable lounge chairs carefully placed at a forty five degree angle to each other. Crossing the room she seats herself on the stepladder stool I use for reaching books on the highest shelf of the bookcase. She looks around without any real interest; a wild animal checking for escape routes. I smile again and gesture to the comfortable chairs.

"Would you like to join me?" I say.

She scowls.

"Nope. Happy here." She crosses her skinny arms over her sunken chest. Her leather shoes were once very good quality. Now they are bound up with masking tape where the sole has come away. I hesitate. Then I wheel my office chair out from behind my desk and roll it towards her. Not too close. She watches me, saying nothing.

"So, how… what brings you here today?" I click my pen and turn over a new page in my A4 notebook, then lay it on my lap. She shrugs and looks out the window. I check my notes nervously. "Um, Silvia, is it?"

"Sylvania," she growls, returning her attention to me.

"Oh, er, sorry." I double check my notes, cross out 'Sylvia' and replace it with 'Sylvania'. She sighs loudly, looking at the ceiling. Her skin is sallow and wrinkled, yet her file says she is only forty one. The lines on her face tell of a hard life. What could carve so deeply into a woman's face and soul?

"Parole conditions," she grumbles.

I nod. "Right. And you're not happy about this, I guess."

"What would you know about it?" She demands, flashing angry grey eyes, flecked with silver at me.

"Well, I…" I clear my throat.

"You," she snarls. "You sit there, *judging* me and you know *nothing* about me, about my life!"

"I try not to make assumptions," I offer.

"You already did!"

"I apologise, Sylvania, I meant no offence." *Going real well, Donna.* I berate myself. *Worth all those years at uni. Good one.* I struggle to think what to say, what to do. I try a different tack. "So, how shall we proceed here? I'm not sure I understand how I can help you."

"Don't need help!" She gets up with a flap of worn clothing and heads for the door.

"Wait!" I call after her. "I have to sign you off on this."

She turns, a scowl of contempt in the one raised eyebrow.

"Is it off or on? Make up your mind."

"Well, I…" *Did she just correct my grammar?* I consult my notes nervously. "Please, just sit down. Wherever you feel comfortable." She remains standing. Just as I'm about to give up she makes her way slowly back to the stool.

"Your file says you were arrested after abducting children." I look up at her briefly. Her facial expression is stony. "Can we talk about that?"

"What's there to say?"

"Well, perhaps the reasons why you felt it necessary to…"

"My business!" Sylvania barks. "No one else's."

"Perhaps the parents of those children, Hansel and Gretel Hauber, wouldn't agree," I say, pragmatically. She mutters and turns away. Her face is red and blotchy. "Did you… feel you were helping these children in some way?" I venture.

"What would you know about it," she mutters, her eyes scanning the office gardens outside; a bleak, featureless lawn edged in concrete with scraggly bushes. Her expression is bleak too.

I press on. "The judge made this order because she thought there was merit in exploring this," I try to explain. "She was giving you another chance." Can't she see this is keeping her from prison? Doesn't she want to avoid a long sentence in that hellhole at Dallingly?

"Judge knows nothing," Sylvania says, then turns to me. I am shocked to see tears, just a hint of them, in her eyes.

"Is it jail time you are afraid of?" I ask gently. *Don't assume! Don't assume, you idiot!* I say to myself. Sylvania clasps and unclasps her hands, stroking her thumb hard. "Was it something about the children you thought you were helping?" I suggest. I scan her history. "You've never been in prison before."

She smiles at me then, an eerie look that makes my skin instantly itchy.

"Never been caught before, have I?"

I swallow. Am I looking at evil here? Clever, cunning, malicious evil? But there is something sad behind her eyes and I want to dig it out and inspect it, see it in the light.

I believe. I have hope.

She folds her arms. "Forget it," she says suddenly.

"Forget what?" I find myself asking.

"About trying to save me."

"I…"

"You're too late. Too far gone."

"But I…"

"The reasons I took those kids you'd never understand."

"You could try me."

"Can't be bothered. Just write in that journal that I'm sorry. Okay?" She gestures irritably at my notebook.

"I don't know if you are."

"What?"

"Sorry."

"Fool!"

"Sorry."

She points at her chest with a triumphant grin. "*I'm* the one who's supposed to be sorry. Ha!"

I can feel my face getting hot. I place the notebook and pen on my desk, get up and push my office chair back behind it. I can feel her eyes upon me, boring into my back. I walk over to the window.

"I often look out at this garden and wonder why someone doesn't make it nicer. It's quite depressing to look at. If the effort was made, it could look lovely. And then bees would be attracted to it, perhaps even little birds," I say.

"Such a perfect little world, isn't it, the one inside your head?" Sylvania says behind me. I turn. Her lips are twisted in a grimace.

"That offends you?"

She shrugs. "Offends me? What the hell do I care?"

"Then why say it?" I challenge her.

"You're so predictable," she says gruffly. "You're all the same."

I regard her, trying to see her with new eyes, a fresh perspective. She's teaching me something. It's important. I know it is. I turn back to the window to think. It's getting noisy in my head lots of voices pushing their points of view, doubt creeping around with its dank cloak. I am feeling a familiar helplessness, that of my nine year old self, struggling to understand my alcoholic mother. Trying to stay safe from her violent hands but needing her love and approval so badly.

"Bad mother," Sylvania says quietly.

I turn. "Pardon?"

"Your mother. Addict was she?"

"How... what..."

"I can see it." She nods to herself. "I can see it," she says softly, looking down at her bony hands. "I've seen that pain before." I blink back tears. *Oh my God, what's happening here? Pull yourself together, Donna! You're the therapist!*

"Is that what you saw in those children?" I say, attempting to corral the conversation to safer territory.

"Go on then, deflect!" She barks. "Drag us back to my so-called crime!"

"But that's why we're here," I say, feeling confidence return. "To talk about you."

She puts her head on the side and regards me hungrily.

"Why should I unburden myself to you, Donna?" She says my name softly. Her grey eyes are older than the mountains where I grew up, older than the river which winds around the valley of this town.

I swallow again, gathering the tatters of my wits together.

"I don't pretend to know all the answers, all the..."

"Yes, you do. You sit there with your notebook and pen and before I even speak you've decided so much about me, based upon your *notes*."

"I have an open mind. I take people as I find them."

"What a noble idea." Sylvania smirks.

"I'm hoping we can find some middle ground here," I say, mentally pushing away an image of myself slapping her.

"Why?" She snaps.

"Well, that's how I usually start. Find something we can agree on."

"How about we agree that you're stupid?" She cackles, slapping her knees.

I give her a patient look. She scowls. I stand up and offer my hand again.

"Thanks for keeping the appointment Sylvania," I say. She stands and regards me.

"Giving up already?" She is swaying slightly. Then her eyes roll into the back of her head and she falls at my feet in a dead faint. I crouch beside her, reaching for her pulse and patting her face. Pulse is flighty and uneven.

"Sylvania! Come on, wake up. Sylvania, can you hear me?" I scramble to my feet and reach for my phone. Seconds later there's a knock on the door. "Come in!" I call. The medical officer arrives with her kit and takes over. A security guard is standing by the door, watching.

"Amazing what these crims will do," he says darkly. "Just to get some sympathy."

"I hardly think this is deliberate!" I say hotly.

He smiles patronisingly.

"She certainly convinced you."

THE FETE
Brenda Slavoff

I shall remember that day all my life. It is as clear to me now, nearly forty years later, as if it were yesterday, and yet . . . yet . . .

I was ten, going on eleven. My grandmother had come to visit us and she took me out specially on my own, as it was the Friday before the September holidays ended. We started out just walking through the familiar parklands of Albert Park Lake, in Melbourne, close to where I lived.

It was mid-morning, a warm spring day, fleecy white clouds across the blue of the sky. Those at the horizon were so thick I said, "They look like snow mountains, don't they?"

Grandma took my hand. "Yes, perhaps if we keep on walking we shall climb them!"

We walked faster, as if it were a game.

Suddenly we arrived at the scene of a carnival. One minute it was quiet, the next there was the towering Ferris wheel and the jingling merry-go-round, the hubbub of eager, happy people, stalls full of handicrafts for sale, the smells of exotic foods, quite unlike the usual carnival fare. There were darling animals on display to judges, and even - more wonderful – equestrian competitions: glossy horses performing show jumps and dressage. For a city girl brought up on National Velvet and horsey books, this was paradise!

"What do you want to look at first?" asked Grandma.

"Oh, everything!"

"Take a few rides first," she suggested, handing me some coins.

"Won't you come too?" She usually handed me on and off.

"No, there's a man I must talk to. See where the seats are? I shall be with him, so you just come back when you're ready."

I was still uncertain. "What if I lose my way?"

"You won't, I'll be watching."

Giving me a kiss on the top of my head, she walked briskly away to join an old gentleman who was dressed in a suit – not very suitable to the occasion – and even a hat. How formal!

That was the moment a boy of about twelve turned up at my elbow with a "Hi there!" of greeting. He had smooth dark hair and a round face, and was dressed in old-fashioned shorts, a knitted vest over a shirt and long checked socks. I studied him and we grinned at each other. He was somehow comfortably familiar but also excitingly unknown – had I gone to the same school with him once, or had one of my sisters? - but it didn't matter enough to ask. With the cheerful ability of children to live fully in the moment we ignored all such unimportant matters and simply fell into friendship.

"Wanna have a look around?"

"Yes," I said, and we trotted off to see the displays.

We played with the dear animals, I talking eagerly about the proper up-bringing of a dog – how I longed for a dog of my own! I knew exactly how to make them happy . . . but my mother never allowed us to have pets. She was too fastidious a housekeeper. We watched the show jumping and took a horse and carriage ride that was doing the rounds. I had never been in a carriage before, and I felt like a grown-up girl in an old fashioned novel. I was glad I was wearing my nice white dress.

My friend's name was David, he said, and he lived with his grandmother. I said I wished I lived with my grandmother too. I thought maybe his parents were dead, and I nearly cried at the thought. But I didn't question him about it. I was just extra nice to him.

We went to the stalls that had games of skill and we both won prizes which we gave to each other. I won a little bear and he a lucky charm. I tied it about my neck, as it was on a ribbon. Then we went on every single ride, some twice. There were even boat rides on the lake and we went in a boat all by ourselves, both of us rowing. When we were out in the middle of the lake it was like being in a different world. David and I talked non-stop about everything around us - we did not talk about school or home life or the future. We bought for lunch food we'd never eaten before and pretended we were exploring a foreign land. Before we left the lakeside, David took out his penknife and we carved our initials in a tree.

After our adventures we returned to my grandmother. She was still sitting in the sun talking to the elderly man. He stood up and smiled as David and I approached, but as far as I can remember said nothing. Oddly I did not introduce David, and Grandma did not inquire who he was. We four strolled about some more, Grandma arm-in-arm with the old man, David and I skipping along together, and we laughed at clowns dressed as medieval jesters and at the open air theatre. At the close of day there was a concert set up on a temporary stage, with a backdrop of golden sunset, and then fireworks as soon as it became dark. What amazing colours and shapes that lived brilliantly for a moment and then faded, almost as soon as they had formed!

As the last wheels of coloured light exploded in the sky, Grandma reached down to hug me and to whisper, "Don't ever forget this day, Iris. Promise me."

I hugged her back. "I won't. Never."

"These days happen so rarely," she murmured, her face lit by the fading glow. "Only when certain circumstances come together. But when they do, you know. They call you."

I didn't know what she meant but I was so happy. I didn't worry about this perfect day ending. I was here, now. That was all that mattered.

Presently Grandma put her hand in mine again and by the light of the now risen moon we walked home. She told me during our walk that I had always been her favourite and she would always be there for me. I felt cherished as I had never been at home.

And there ends the memory of that happy day, for I cannot recall what happened after we returned home, what my mother said, or when Grandma left.

I never saw her again.

The following Sunday morning came the phone call to tell us that Grandma had passed away.

Many years later I happened to mention the wonderful day I had spent with Grandma at the carnival, two days before her passing away. I had never forgotten it.

"It's impossible," said Mum. "Gran was too ill before she died to visit anyone. Aunt Elizabeth was staying with her. She certainly couldn't have been rushing around as you say she did. You must be confusing it with the time she took you to the zoo."

To my astonishment no one else could remember her coming to visit us close to the time she died.

"But it happened!" I insisted. "And it wasn't the zoo. It was a sort of carnival or fete and there were rides and horses. I rowed on the lake. And I was so excited because John Farnham was singing at the concert. And another group sang the old Seekers' song, 'The Carnival is over.'"

My father and sisters declared it could not have happened. There would not have been equestrian displays in such a city park. I was mixing it up with Moomba, with all its floats and displays.

"But Moomba's at the wrong time of the year," I protested. "This was springtime, there were blossoms everywhere."

"There aren't any blossoming trees at that park," said Kim, my eldest sister.

That was true. But it was a minor detail.

"I brought home a lucky charm a boy gave me. It was a pendant."

"I don't remember you ever having such a thing," said my second sister Barbara, "and we shared rooms then."

What had happened to it? Though I searched everywhere, I couldn't find it. I thought affectionately of David. I remembered going home with Grandma but not saying goodbye to David – or the old gentleman, for that matter. Childlike, I had never thought of the future, or to ask David where he lived or whether we'd meet again.

"Maybe we took photos," I said desperately. I brought out all the old albums and went through them carefully. No photos of this happiest day of my childhood! Then I saw a pile of loose photos at the bottom of the cupboard. So unusual for my mother not to have put them carefully away. Amongst these photos was a picture of Grandma and an old gentleman. I started up triumphantly. There in the picture was the gentleman she had been talking to that day, I was sure of it . . . dressed in a suit and with a hat, even! The background, however, was of a house I had never seen, and Grandma looked younger, maybe in her sixties; while he looked the same age as I had seen him. So they were friends. Excitedly I waved the photo, "That's the man Grandma was talking to at the carnival!"

"That's my father," said my mother, only looking briefly at the photo and putting it aside, "your grandfather. You only ever saw him as a baby, for he died when you were six months old. He was older than Gran."

I'd known Grandpa had died when I was a baby, and I suppose I must have seen his pictures at some time. Yet I couldn't believe that the man Grandma had talked to at the fete didn't exist. Maybe he just looked similar, and that's why she liked him.

In the years to come I was to go through all the possibilities. Had I imagined it all, as a hotchpotch of separate events? Had it been a particularly vivid dream? Was it wishful thinking? I had been only ten after all, and everyone else was older and presumably better able to remember and judge. Yet somehow I could not dismiss that day. I *knew* it had happened. It was the most significant day of my childhood, because for that one day everything had been perfect; it had been like a homecoming. And at that time of my life I had been going through a very stressful period. Six months previously I had been hit by a car and had had my leg in plaster. I had begun to need glasses to see the blackboard at school, and was at the point of needing braces, too, and was dreading the necessary extraction of four teeth for this. Yet I couldn't remember wearing my glasses to see in the distance on that particular day, not even when trying to get the ball in the fake clowns' mouths. Nothing had worried me that day.

Maybe I got the year wrong? That was possible. Obviously it could not have been later, as Grandma had died when I was ten, but could it have occurred before these bad events? When I was nine? No; for I distinctly remember Grandma dying two days later. I remember thinking, 'Thank you, God, for letting me see her just before she died,' but I had not said so to anyone else.

For a long time the feeling persisted that she wasn't dead, that if I went back to those parklands I might see her again. I had often imagined, during those troubled childhood times, myself wandering away into that enchanted day again, somehow, somewhere, and living an everlasting perfect day. Why had we come home at all? Why hadn't we just stayed there, together, Grandma and me?

The memory haunted me. Was it real or had it never happened?

Of course, my ordinary life went on. High school, college, teaching. I taught English, English Literature as my preference. I loved to stimulate the imagination of the kids. "It's a real world if you believe in it," I say of the novels. "The characters become your friends, and you take part in their creation. In stories you can learn things you cannot from ordinary life."

One day while visiting Mum and Dad, I decided to go for a walk. It was sunset and there would be a full moon. A sudden urge gripped me to go to the parklands, a fearful excitement; as though I were an electric wire through which too much power were singing. Was it calling me? Yes.

I hurried all the way there, my heart thudding. I knew that in my soul I longed for some wonderful recurrence of that time, that I would stumble upon perfection, maybe stay there this time. I had been to these parks since that time, with family and once on a date to the restaurant, but everything felt different now.

I entered the cool grassy areas. Part had been swallowed in a carpark, and I had forgotten about the golf courses. I wandered among the trees, still lit by the sunset glow.

There were people about still, some going to the sports complexes, while cars droned past, not far away, around the lake, making fairy lights on the still water.

I came to the edge of the lake. Yes, it was here that David and I had returned the boat, and stood talking. And surely – surely, it was on one of these trees that we had carved our initials?
Which was it? Here, a smooth-barked native tree. It had grown in thirteen years. I crouched down and ran my fingers over the bark, to the height of a child. There was an irregularity in its smooth surface. I peered down and read: "D and I." And under that, "I and D." I vividly remembered writing it twice so that both of us could have our initial first.

But this couldn't be, after so many years, in a growing tree! The carving looked re-done. Someone else's initials? I stared at the carving, satisfied at last in the wonder and miracle of life, as the full moon peeped over the horizon.

THE SLEEPING PRINCESS WAKES
Brenda Slavoff

Part I.

When the Sleeping Princess opened her eyes
To rosy clouds at eastern skies,
Their midnight depths so awoke with light
That sleepy warmth was chilled with dawn.
She thought she'd feel the touch of loving sight
Ere she had uttered one contented yawn,
But brightening glow awakened her to day,
And made her see the room in which she lay.

Confusion touched her quickening senses shrill;
Her heart was stricken down with icy chill.
"What," muffled senses cried aghast,
"What musty room is this where I repose?
Oh, do I lie in death that was the past?
I was content to sleep, to dream I chose -
No other choice had I but dark-faced death.
I found my youth too warm for such cold breath.

"Yet he breathes now in this cold ante-room
Of all that was, and is, of shuttered gloom!
Oh where are friends and family, where are foes?
I thought to wake up to my smiling prince,
Why am I desolate amidst such woes?
How many loves and losses have passed since?
For ten long decades I have dreamed for this!
Death mastered me when I had hoped for bliss!

"Look at the shuttered window there!
See outside my room - all bare!
No life now stirs, I cannot hear a voice!
Cold dungeons could not ever be worse.
Why am I here, or did I have a choice?
That witch who uttered loud the curse,

Does she live still, and does the one
Who promised good ere life was done?

"Remember, how I thought myself above,
Apart from all the rest, the peaceful dove?
My destiny to offend the bad,
Did never make me sad.
A hundred years have passed for me
Since I did take the wrong path free,
And now in fear I dread this night,
This dawn, this day, of life's own might.

"I have been dreaming all the while I slept,
I have been busy, my soul in faith I kept -
But I am just a tool of careless Fate,
Of fairies' whims, and Chance's cruel mandate.
I see so clearly how things might have been,
They are more real than all the things I've seen!
Now I am never to be crowned to rule,
I am forgotten here, in restless longing cruel!

"I do not know what path to take,
I did it for the witch, and for the fairy's sake,
And now they have forgotten all they said,
And I in state do lie upon an empty bed
Of dust, and memories that never lived,
Unmade by man, by priest unshrived.
I thought that everyone in faith would keep
Their memory of me whilst I did sleep.

"Oh I suppose my weeping friends did go their way,
To marry, live and die for their brief day;
All dead, and I asleep, my deeds unseen;
No smiling prince, no maids - and I a queen,
Of futility, of waste, of useless love!
There is an Ark nowhere for this tired dove."

Part II.

Not until noon did she her hand entreat
To pull aside the shutter at the windowseat.
Not yet a sound but hinges crying out
From silence, through the hush of mounds of dust.
Her footsteps showing sadly as in doubt,
As pitiful and wretched as the rust. Her touch
On bed, on window shutter's smear,
Oh such a place is haunted just by fear!

"Why did I raise myself to this?
There is no life, just death there is...."
      "Yet open the window, let in the lark,
      She flies so far, must she now brave the dark?
      You are the maker of the Ark,
      You are the chooser of the mark!"
"What voice is this?" the princess cried,
And suddenly rose to the window's side.
"Oh open, then! The window's wide!
There goes the wind - so where is pride?

"I stand now in a ruinous waste; time is unkind.
Life is to face me, alone, childhood so far behind.
I cannot speak of it and not find tears -
A hundred - a hundred - years!
I am too frightened to search for life,
I must stay here, whose decades sheltered me,
Remain, where once I live a life,
Another hundred years - I'll not be free!

"Never, never to see a face,
Never, never to leave this place.
Oh Fate, why have you closed me in this tomb
I thought was Life's own gentle womb?
I cannot be born to love, to answer - why?
I am forsaken, frightened - let me die!

"If I outlive these walls - what then?

Another year will come, again, again.
Should I remain and watch these walls' slow crumbling,
This roof's pride humbling,
   gates, stones, towers tumbling -?
Oh do not die, my palace, pity me!
You are my youth, my past, my eternity,
My one and only solace!
I am queen of just this palace.

"What will I do, where will I go -
For though the walls' decay is slow,
Yet will I still endure when death claims all
And spiders spin their webs as palls -
I wonder, should I wait for someone's tread,
Stay here in dread - or go alone
Out of these sorrowing halls of the dead,
Or is it mad to leave my throne?

"Remember how I used to study hard
My lessons, to be tested on some day?
Oh, that I were at one such test now
Instead of here, debating now the way!
I was not tested for such things,
Was never taught to acquire wings,
I have no place where I can turn,
What is the knowledge that I did not learn?

"Even if my prince came - what of that?
He could be taken from me, in some way,
Disillusion assailing me; I have no arms for that.
And now the sunset steals away my day....
I do not believe in fairies' magic now,
In spirits, miracles, and wondrous joy -
It was not writ that I should suffer more!
Believe now? How!

Life, if you came to me in my own prince
And I live in peace, forgetting all,
How would it armour me against cold chance

Or Fate herself? My warmth would be my pall.
Let me not dance!"

PART III.

The wind blows shrill; it blows from whence?
A graveyard, or the church incense?
"Oh tell me where blow dandelion seeds
When they are scattered by the breeze?
Release from my full heart the hopes not killed,
Go where you will, my blossoms, be fulfilled!
Gone is strife, she fled with all the rest,
May I now pray for peace and find it blessed,
Between my hands in supplication pressed?

"Oh tender wind, a breeze so fresh and fair,
How do you dare?
Blowing this dust like any fragrant grass,
Don't you know it will not pass?
A breeze from the meadows, are you so?
From towering mountains capped with snow,
From flowery leas, blue tranquil seas -?
Oh breeze! So free, you do as you please,
Don't touch my hair, release it from your spell,
Nor swirl the dead-leaf pattern at my feet -
For I am far too old for your youth sweet;
Too cold to bear your breath so well,
Too young for you to not bestir my blood!

"Here is a leaf, a live one, and a twig,
Two petals of the rose, and now a sprig
Of jasmin, blown from far away....
So far away from these lost, dying walls,
Crumbling down like wood to ashes charred;
My vision's struck, my palace marred,
As if fire supreme and unendurable,
Had opened to admit the outer world. They fall!
My night has faded. Day appears!
So quickly has it happened, what I feared!

"I ask myself, what if it had been real
What I had feared would pass with them?
Instead of balm to heal, a greater loss?
But that can never be, the fairy promised,
Fears and trials will pass into the day."

PART IV.

"I thought the fire was dead that lit my soul,
A sacrificial fire within the votary's bowl,
Now phoenix-like it shakes the ashes of its former state,
Scattered as upon the requiem-plate -

"I did not die - no, I was sent black-masked
To view the underworld of all my past;
What could I see but black? What had I held but lack?
How could I ask grim Hades to send me back
To sunshine's gold, when I had grown so old?

"So hold me now towards my life's embrace!
Let me gaze enraptured at his face!
And while I gaze I hear the beat of music
Straining, surging, shouting triumph's song!
What have I learned - to live!
What have I lost - not lost, I give!
Sure knowledge of all fear I've gained....
Now take me far, far from this place!

"A procession that lives is coming for me now,
And he whom I was promised leads the way....
Let night's pale moon bow to the day,
She who has conquered death now lives,
She who was promised love beholds her prince!"

ALL THE BIRDS ARE SAYING GOODNIGHT
Dawn Meredith

The warmth of day folds into night,
A feathery softness of lingering light.
The cool of the dark is a soothing balm,
The sweetness of dew so restful and calm.

The sun is shy now, hiding her face.
Her sister the moon is taking her place.
The silvery stars all twinkle and glow
As we settle down, sleepy, on the Earth below.

All the birds are saying goodnight,
Cheeping softly in pale pink light,
Beaks tucked neatly under their wing,
Dreaming of morning songs they'll sing.

Tiny honey-eater and Frog-mouth Owl,
Sharp-eyed eagle and Malleefowl,
Splendid Wren and Superb Fruit Dove,
Rosella and parrot, in treetops above.

Long-billed Corella and Square-tailed kite,
Satin Bowerbird as black as the night.
Kingfisher, butcherbird, whistler and lark,
Finch and scrubwren twitter in the dark.

And now, my little Nightjar, little Emerald Dove,
Snuggle down, safe in my downy love.
A warm, gentle hug, a velvety kiss,
Flutter away lightly, on wings of bliss.

Soar with the osprey in moonlight beams,
Chit-chit with the warblers in sunlit streams.
Dive with the Rockhopper penguins in the sea,
But always return to your nest here with me.

GOING WEST
Allan Jamieson

I'd be lying if I stated that today started like any other day. Two reasons will convince you, I'm sure.

First, the date: January 1. In my life, I've experienced only 79 days having that date. Secondly, it is not often, anywhere, that the midday meal on New Year's Day comprises a whole Tasmanian sea-cray (lobster, to those living elsewhere) accompanied by a soup comprising Japanese tofu and seaweed. The combination could, I reckon, classify the day as genuinely unique.

What's more, it was warm and sunny with a weak, westerly wind and the sea was almost mirror-like when I viewed it through the large glass windows of my beach-side shack. This weather was certainly wonderful and you can't always claim that in these parts during the Christmas-New Year holiday period.

I'd just consumed two-thirds of a bottle of superb Australian Riesling (Tahbilk's if you're wondering) and – right now – I'm sitting in my favourite armchair, reclined, contemplating the high pine-wood-lined cathedral ceiling of the shack, nestled within the Rocky Cape National Park.

Bliss? Lucky bastard? I'll admit to that – BUT! The mail in my Burnie PO box yesterday included one letter in with an assortment of delayed Christmas cards. I've only now got around to looking at the envelope, after the crayfish lunch and after the immediate impact of the alcohol had worn off. Half sober, I realised that I was in deep trouble – so deep, I sobered up instantly.

I recognised the handwriting and the postmark showed he was in Tasmania too, not half a world away, where I'd hoped he would stay. The letter had been posted before Christmas. He'd evidently spent some time tracking me down, though Google makes searches fairly easy these days. Pity! When I managed to evade him and get away, the worldwide web was a mere figment of somebody's imagination.

He had caught up to me.

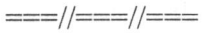

"Do you know where he might be?" It was the fourth time I'd approached a stranger in Burnie, mentioned his name and then followed a positive response with this second question.

"Maybe; he told me some years ago that he always spent the Christmas-New Year weeks at his shack, to get away from everybody. It's at Sisters Beach, 30 minutes' drive from here. I recall him saying he doesn't have the phone on, so you'll have to go there if you want to talk with him. Can I ask if he's done something?"

"No, it's just that I haven't seen him in years. I'm in Australia for the first time and I thought I'd look him up."

"Where are you from?"

"Brazil."

"*Brazil!* I never knew he'd been there!"

"Oh yes, he was there once upon a time."

"Well, I'll be blowed – just goes to show. You learn something every day."

"Yes, thanks for your help."

"Oh, that's OK – happy hunting!"

I turned and walked around the corner to where my rental-car was parked. Finding him hadn't been too hard. My adviser back home was right; Tasmanians *are* close-knit and everyone seemed to know everybody else. Well, almost; everyone knew his name, but it was only this last bloke who could suggest where he might be hiding. It fitted. He had reason to keep a low profile. Tasmania was about as far away from everywhere as he could wish, but he hadn't done enough to hide from the Tasmanians. Perhaps the remoteness of the island fooled him into letting his guard down. It had been many years, after all.

I searched my road map and found Sisters Beach. Starting the engine, I turned to the west.

===//===//===

Where was he? He could be close, or he probably would be soon. No time to waste; I cleaned up the residue from that lunch, tipped the last drops from the wine bottle, and made the shack appear genuinely vacated. Into my car I stacked everything I hastily thought could be useful, closed the boot and drove away.

Had he found out what car I drove? Better not assume "no". I drove to the end of a side street, dumped the car and walked off, loaded down with the "essentials" and climbed the path up to the true Rocky Cape Park – walking tracks only, no cars – and there I paused.

Turning, I could look down on my shack from about 700 m away. I sat and waited. Would he make a visit there today? If not, tomorrow? I felt a bit like Richard Hannay, on the run from those who wanted him killed, as he roamed the Scottish highlands while able to spy the goings-on down below him on the road.

It was almost dark; the sun was setting behind me as I sat and watched my shack. Maybe, in half an hour it would be too dark; then suddenly a car approached, its lights already aglow, and turned into my property.

Even from this distance, I recognised him. Knocking on the door, he waited – and waited. Then he moved to look in the windows before reappearing and knocking once more.

Maybe five minutes was all it took and then he drove off.

I was wary. I decided to sleep up here, just off the walking track, and see what tomorrow would bring. Luckily the weather held and I managed a few hours' sleep.

I gazed again at my shack. No movement! My gut feel told me to be ultra-careful; if he'd come all the way from Brazil, he would be unlikely to give up searching quite so easily. For the next few days – and nights – he'd probably re-visit my shack.

What to do? I decided to walk to the other end of the Park, some 3 or 4 hours away. From there, I reckoned I could thumb a lift to wherever that driver was heading. It was simply too hazardous to believe I could regain the use of my shack.

Damn! Those first few hours of 2019 held out great promise, but now I knew I had to move. Where? How?

Picking up my haversack, I trudged off to the west. This year would be a Big Unknown.

Jan. 3

I made it as far as Strahan yesterday. At the western end of the National Park, I hardly had to wait at all before a bloke in a battered old utility stopped.

"Where are you going?" he said. "Wherever you're heading, or until you're tired of my company" I replied.

He laughed, I got in and we went as far as Smithton. He was a farmer and had to collect a pump before returning home. I asked him to drop me off close to where the Western Explorer road started. To me, this route offered a way of travelling with a very low chance of being recognised by anybody, but I *was* taking a gamble that someone would want to drive along that road *and* would be prepared to pick up a hitchhiker. My luck was in! After walking about five k's, a car stopped and I was soon heading south in a 4WD Toyota driven by a young bloke from England who was touring Tasmania with his girlfriend. She was from Canada. I was fortunate, I reckoned, that they had only been a few days on the island and would be unlikely to ask any troublesome questions – though questions did come.

In effect, we were all tourists, because I had never travelled on this road, though I could explain its history to the two adventurers in the front seats. It's not an overly exciting road, but it does provide an alternative route from Smithton to the West Coast towns of Strahan and Queenstown than does the long-established highway.

Turning to look at me from the front seat, the girl said, "you're a bit old to be thumbing a ride, aren't you?" Before I could answer, the driver added, "yes, we figured an old fellow would be less likely to do us harm."

A slight smile formed on my face; the bloke from Brazil was about my age and he could still cause me great harm – age was no sure safeguard.

"Fair question; in fact, this is the first time I've done any hitchhiking since I was your age. I'm well and truly retired nowadays and have no ties and no deadlines. I could have driven my car to Strahan, but the weather forecast was too promising to ignore – the West Coast gets a huge amount of rain, even in summer, and the prospect of a week of fine weather was something to savour. I like walking and I was prepared to walk the whole way if nobody stopped to offer me a lift." I hoped this rather lengthy response would cut out some other questions that might seem obvious to curious tourists.

For the rest of the journey, we chatted about odds and sods and nothing arose of a consequential nature. They were both city people and the idea of walking for fun, miles away from traffic lights, struck them as an absurd concept – too absurd to be even mildly curious about.

I feel safe here at Strahan, though I felt safe at Sisters Beach too, so obviously safety is relative.

It was just 45 years ago that I left Brazil. I'd had enough of that very dangerous country, especially its cities Sao Paulo and Rio de Janeiro. Back then, Brazil was controlled by a military dictatorship; you'd reckon this would ensure the Law was strong, but *lawful* was an unknown word there. For instance, Brazil is (or *was*):

- where every man who wears a hat also wears a gun. Those who wear berets either wear two guns or one gun plus a 50 cm long baton. Some men have dispensed with the hat. If they are police, they will be found standing along highways every 20 km or so, or every 20 blocks in cities; standing, half leaning as if they were being supported by an invisible electric light pole. Most shaved the day before yesterday! Ordinary men (i.e., those without hats and guns) go to great lengths to avoid contact with these upholders of the law.
- where most shops that rate a glass display window facing the street, also rate protection by depraved Clint Eastwood lookalikes lounging in the doorway, hands on gun holsters. Who or what are they protecting? Banks usually have two of these characters ever-ready to attract custom to the bank by directing their spit away from you.
- where ordinary citizens driving their cars home at night don't stop at stop lights for fear of being robbed or kidnapped at gunpoint in their own car.
- where a man with a beret (remember them?) decides to escort you to a place where you can change your US dollars but where you will not get a receipt that will allow you to convert back unused cruzeiros on departure.
- where the sole official money exchange at Rio de Janeiro International Airport is on the third floor of the domestic terminal, but *you* have arrived from your overseas flight on the ground floor of the international section of the terminal. Hence the prevalence of helpful men wearing berets.

Why did this bloke try to hunt me down? Simply because I was not

– and never will be – Brazilian. I mean, I behaved in what I believed would be the proper, civilised way to behave in <u>any</u> country. Unfortunately, in Brazil that attitude is guaranteed to get you into trouble, yea even murdered!

It was a September morning when I witnessed a violent confrontation on Avenida Ipiranga, not far from Hotel Excelsior, where I was staying. An innocent man – so I thought – was set upon by two men and one drew a gun and shot the man. The thugs turned to run and ran into me, as I was running to help the wounded man. The thug with the gun shouted at me in Portuguese, pointing the gun at me for good measure. I moved to push past the pair to reach the man on the footpath.

"What's your f— in' name, mister?" I turned, looked at him and said, "what's it to you?"

They broke away, crossed the road and turned into a side street, just seconds before an unmarked Ford transit van pulled up beside me. From the back sprang five men, each one wearing a light grey uniform with a dark grey beret and holding a sub-machinegun. They surrounded me; Federal Police – hand-picked for the job – each man was over six foot tall and well-built. Even without their guns, you'd have to be a fool, or drunk, or both, to pick a fight with any one of them.

I pointed to the side street and said, "the two thugs went that way." One policeman asked me my name and then ran to follow his mates, who had already turned up the side street.

I looked at the man on the ground. He was moaning, so hadn't been fatally shot. I tried to comfort him, until I saw a familiar sight – a black VW Beetle. It stopped and two uniformed men (with berets) got out. These were the local police. They examined the poor fellow before picking him up and managing, with some difficulty, half pulling, half pushing to squeeze him into the back of their police car and drive away, but not before I'd been asked my name – for the third time in less than three minutes. Everything had gone like a whirlwind; I'd had no time to think. Given half a moment to gather my thoughts, I would instinctively have turned away, like any ordinary Brazilian would.

I should have, but I hadn't and the consequences were soon upon me. The next day, the Federal police took me to a prison, where they asked me to identify the gunman. That I did, though this gave him a chance to confirm what I looked like – and call me a snitch. I felt like a rabbit caught in a spotlight.

The upshot? The thug was sentenced to 12 months gaol, but not before he'd heard my name during the court proceedings. From prison he sent me a letter, vouching to hunt me down no matter where I might hide.

It seemed obvious that information of any kind had a value in Brazil, especially in criminal circles, and that wherever I went in Brazil, eventually someone would recognise me.

It was time to leave Brazil.

I had opened that envelope – he *claimed* he wanted to apologise. Now it is time for me to leave Tasmania also. Where to this time?

MEMORIES
Lesley Podmore - 2007

Clear swirls of gentle light-touched ripples,
    My feet a-swash
    A-plosh   a-plosh.
    Sand moves ------ light flashes --------- small fish fly,
    A-swash   a-swash.

My heart is joyous in this place;
    My soul settles into peace.
    I hold it all within my heart.
    A memory now
    A memory ever

Always here.

AN INTERESTING CHALLENGE:
To find the whereabouts of a Japanese soldier
Allan Jamieson

I was aware that many Italian prisoners of war had been allowed to work in Tasmania during the Second World War, but in June 2014, my wife Kuniko and I were challenged by a Burnie Rotarian: Could we locate the whereabouts of the owner of a Japanese army cap in the Rotarian's possession?

Then 88 years old, the Rotarian was Noel Atkins, who told of how he came to meet a Japanese soldier near Launceston during the war, at which time Noel was in Scouts. His Scout troop befriended the young soldier, who gave Noel his cap.

Noel had a long and notable career as a school teacher and headmaster, as well as being a state level footballer in Tasmania and football coach (he taught the outstanding footballer Darryl Baldock how to play). I had known Noel for fifteen years and we had always enjoyed tossing questions to each other to challenge the mind.

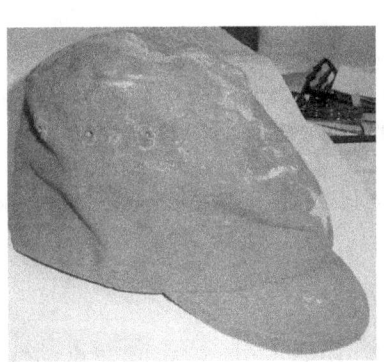 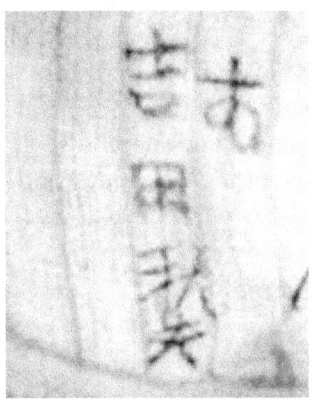

吉田　　秋夫

The name in the cap was that of Yoshida Akio san. Yoshida is a rather common surname in Japan so, in addition to the long time that had passed since the war, this challenge of Noel's was not a small one! I was conscious of four possible endings:

1.　　The cap did not belong to the soldier Noel had met – thus any search based on the name Yoshida Akio san would be a red herring

2.   There might have been several POWs with name Yoshida Akio san – thus sorting out *now* which one Noel had met could be impossible if all these men had passed away

3.   I might not be able to find any information on a POW called Yoshida Akio san

4.   There was only one POW called Yoshida Akio san and it was he who handed his cap to Noel.

I looked first for information on the New Guinea campaign, as it seemed most likely that the soldier had fought and been captured in this area. I found *Japanese Army Operations in the South Pacific Area – New Britain and Papua campaigns, 1942-1943*. The author, Dr Steven Bullard (Senior Historian at the Australian War Museum), had translated the Japanese army records relating to this area of conflict. I noted from his biography on the AWM website that Bullard's 'recent research interests include the experience of … Japanese prisoners of war in Australia'. While engrossed in reading his most interesting book, I decided to contact him. My email of 10 July to Dr Bullard read in part:

> My friend knows that I visit Japan every year, so he is hoping I can trace this soldier or his descendants. I wondered if you are aware of any files or records which might contain names and/or army regiment identifications of Japanese prisoners in Australia, *especially* of any who ended up in Tasmania – ideally if the names are in kanji.

Steven's reply:

> I am not aware of a POW camp in Tasmania, or records dealing with those POWs allowed working on farms, but the National Archives of Australia holds various other records relating to Japanese prisoners of war and internees. You can search for the name of the soldier at: http://recordsearch.naa.gov.au but note that many POWs gave false names.

I chose to start my research on the NAA website. There were 31 files for POWs with the surname Yoshida, but only <u>one</u> for Yoshida Akio san. I inspected the digitised details for him. There was no mention of him being in Tasmania, but there was a period (between August

1944 and March 1946) when his whereabouts were not detailed in these online records.

Report on Internee			
ID PWJA (USA) 147028	Surname Yoshida	Other names Akio	Nationality Japanese
Date of Birth	3 Aug 1920		
Place of birth: Yamagami mura, Aza Fuumaki, Hino gun, Tottori ken		Priv. address: Tottori ken, Hino gun, Yamagami mura, Aza Fukumaki	
Occupation	Farmer		
Religion	Sodoshu (Buddhist)		
Place of capture	Gurishi (New Britain)		
Date of capture	13 Feb. 1944	Date of internment	28 April 1944
Height 5' 5"	Weight 130	Complexion Sallow	Hair black
Eyes brown	Marks:	Mortar shrapnel wound, back of left knee	
Medical exam.?	Yes	Personal effects	Nil
Married or Single	Unmarried	Next of kin: Father	Yoshida Yuji
Service Rank:	Sgt 53 Regt, 17 Div, 2 Bn, 5 Coy		

==//==

International Relief Bureaux		
Place of internment	Cowra, NSW	

==//==

Property statement - POW			
	(Signed)	吉 田 秋 夫	8 May 1944

==//==

Transport Form				
Date	From whom		Date	Place
3.5.44	Qld L of C	Marched into Gaythorne (ex. SWPA)	18.4.44	Gaythorne
31.5.44	"	Marched out to Cowra	20.5.44	"

7.6.44	NSW L of C	Marched in to Cowra	22.5.44	Cowra
6.6.44	"	Marched in to 15 ACH (Malar-ia)	22.5.44	"
30.6.44	"	Rejoined camp (ex. hosp.)	25.5.44	"
25.9.44	"	Trans. To Murchison	30.8.44	"
11.9.44	Mur-chison	Marched in ex. Cowra	31.8.44	Murchison
4.3.46	Vic L of C	Marched out and embarked *Daikai Maru*		Sydney

At this point, I implored upon Noel the need for him to recall <u>when</u> he met the soldier. I wanted to know the year, but I did not reveal what I had discovered, because it could be that 'my' Yoshida san was not the same as the one he met.

By August 1944, there were 2,223 Japanese POWs in Australia, including 544 merchant seamen and many others due to their being born in Japan or married to a Japanese person. There were also 14,720 Italian prisoners, who had been captured mostly in the North African Campaign, and 1,585 Germans, mostly naval or merchant seamen.

The Cowra breakout

Cowra, a farming district about 300km west of Sydney, was the town nearest to No. 12 Prisoner of War Compound, a major POW work camp, where 4,000 Axis military personnel and civilians were detained. The camp was the site of one of the largest prison escapes of the war.

In the first week of August 1944, a tip-off from an informer at Cowra led authorities to plan a move of all Japanese POWs at Cowra, except officers and NCOs, to another camp at Hay, New South Wales, some 400km to the west. The Japanese were notified of the move on 4 August.

On 5 August, 545 Japanese attempted escape: 231 of them and four Australian soldiers died during the uprising. The surviving escapees were recaptured. In the 68 page report by the Authorities (on the NAA website) I could read:

AMF COMPANY COMPOUND
No.1 Vickers Gun
NORTH
X No.2 Vickers Gun
MAIN GATES
B. JAPANESE
COWRA TOWNSHIP
(3.2 KM S.W)
A sketch of the four compounds at the POW camp.
BROADWAY
A. ITALIANS
NO MANS LAND
C. ITALIANS
D. JAPANESE OFFICERS/ FORMOSANS, KOREANS!
AMF COMPANY COMPOUND
● Towers
➤ Breakout points
AMF COMPANY COMPOUND
0   75   150 METRES

Of the 230 fatalities, 20 died by hanging and strangulation inflicted by the Japanese on each other or by themselves, nine suicided by stabbing and two ran under a train. Also twelve bodies were found in the five huts burnt by the Japanese. Sixteen of the wounded showed signs of attempted suicide.

Japanese prisoners of war feared the worst when they returned to Japan after the war. For the most part, their fears went unrealized, and they were able to reintegrate into Japanese society relatively smoothly. One ex-POW even rose to flag rank in the post-war Japanese Maritime Self-Defence Force.

All surviving Japanese POWs – eye witnesses of the breakout – were quickly transferred away from Cowra. On 31 August 1944, Yoshida san arrived at the Murchison camp (20 km south of the town of Tatura in central Victoria).

Tatura camps

There were seven camps in the Tatura area during World War II which held about 4,000-8,000 people at any one time. Three camps housed POWs; the remaining four camps held internees who were civilians living in Australia or other Allied territories and countries at the outbreak of war and were deemed to be a security risk because of their nationality. The camps were situated in the Goulburn Valley, where food and water were plentiful.

It is unclear what happened to Yoshida san between August 1944 and March 1946 when the records show he was placed on the *Daikai Maru* for repatriation to Japan – thus he *might* have been in the Launceston area for some of this time.

The Argus (Melbourne), Thursday 28 February 1946 page 1

SYDNEY, Wed: The Japanese steamer *Daikai Maru*, from Kobe, passed through the heads this morning. She will repatriate 2,691 POW's from New South Wales. The vessel has a displacement of only 3,500 tons, and the POW's will be uncomfortably crowded.

In August, while Kuniko and I were in Melbourne, Kuniko noticed a short article in the local Japanese language newspaper, *Nichigo Press*. This stated that a Murakami Teruo san had arrived in Australia to attend the 70th anniversary of the Cowra breakout. He was accompanied by an interpreter, Yamada Mami san. I immediately 'Googled' their names, and found:

- Murakami san (an army private), now 93 years old, was the last surviving member of the Japanese who escaped from Cowra capable of making the visit. During the breakout, he sheltered in a ditch until found, when he readily surrendered.
- Yamada Mami san was revealed to be an extraordinarily active writer with a truly staggering list of topics, including *Lost Officer* about the Cowra breakout. I resolved to contact her in regard to my challenge.

Kuniko and I considered making a visit to 'my' Yoshida san's home town in Tottori Prefecture during our annual trip to Japan (October 2014).

Below is the exchange of emails with Yamada Mami san on August 11.

2014-08-11 8:59 GMT+09:00:
To Yamada Mami san
Please excuse my contacting you 'cold' without an introduction. In late June this year, my wife (Kuniko) and I were given a very difficult challenge: to locate the descendants (if any) of a Japanese soldier who was a POW in Cowra during the breakout. I attach more about why we were given the challenge, and also showing what we have discovered so far.
We will be in Japan from 16 October to 30 October this year and we would like to try and make contact with a descendant if possible. Do you know of any records or organisations which might be of help to us?
Allan Jamieson Burnie, Tasmania
===//===
From: Yamada Mami
Sent: Monday, August 11, 2014 11:10 AM
To: Allan
Subject: Re: Yoshida challenge - re. Cowra
Dear Allan,
Have just read your email. Nice to hear from you. Actually it took a minute for me to locate Mr. Akio Yoshida. I know his actual name and his present mailing address. I am not sure if he keeps well nowadays, but I can at least talk to his family (or himself if I am lucky) regarding your letter.
Could you tell me what you exactly would like? Do you wish to return his cap to him?
Mami
===//===
2014-08-11 13:38 GMT+09:00:
My hope is to be able to return the cap to Yoshida Akio san or to his descendants. His 94th birthday would have been last week (3 August), if he is still alive.
Allan Jamieson
===//===
From: Yamada Mami
Sent: Monday, August 11, 2014 2:47 PM
To: Allan
Subject: Re: Yoshida challenge - re. Cowra
Allan-san,

I have found out that Akio Yoshida has already passed away. (Sorry about that.). I can ask his bereaved family if they want to see you and your wife when you visit Japan later this year. (Do you want me to check?)

Mami

===//===

Yes, please ask. My wife and I do not want to put his family to any trouble and our visit would be friendly and very brief. Please say we are sorry to learn of his passing. We could post the cap to his home if we have the address.

Allan Jamieson

I discovered that another person with the name Yoshida Akio san was in the School of Medicine at Tottori University. I was able to email him and on August 12, I received his reply:

I am not a descendant nor have I any information about your Akio Yoshida. Yamamagamimura is now one area in a small town called Nichinan-cho. So I think that several relatives of Mr. Yoshida are still living in that town. I am forwarding your email and attached files to the town office. Maybe they can help you. I made a comparison between the two signatures. I feel that these signatures were written by different persons, because the first kanji differs; in one case the longer horizontal line is at top but in the other case it is at the bottom. People whose name is Yoshida are strict in this difference.

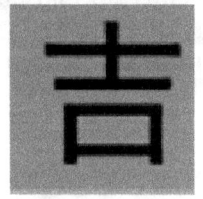 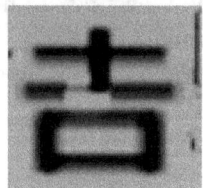

On August 11, I had spoken with Noel at our Rotary club meeting. All along, he had believed that he must have met the Japanese soldier in late 1942; the reason being that in January 1943 he commenced his first teaching job on King Island and hence he was not in Launceston after that date. I pointed out to Noel that he recalled the meeting taking place in summertime (December or January) when all schools would have been on vacation. Thus, I suggested, Noel went home to Launceston during the vacation period and would have resumed contact with his friends, including possibly those from the Scout troop. Noel agreed that this *could* have happened, in which case the meeting could have taken place in late 1945 or in January 1946 when Noel was 20 years old and "my" Yoshida san was 25 years old.

Another Burnie Rotarian learned of my apparent success and, when I mentioned Cowra, she said her father had performed guard duty on trains bringing Japanese prisoners to Cowra. Her father said the guards had rifles but no bullets!

This prompted me to concoct this theory:

> After the war ended in August 1945, perhaps Yoshida san was able to leave the camp *if* accompanied by an Australian soldier or some other guardian; maybe he had made friends with a Tasmanian soldier. The date of the meeting with Noel must then have been approximately January 1946.

I cannot conceive of any other explanation as to how the Japanese soldier came to be in Tasmania.

I did not receive any further communication from Yamada Mami san, so on August 29, Kuniko and I emailed the Nichinan Town Office to describe our Challenge and to seek information on any relatives of Yoshida san. On September 2, we received a reply, which said in effect:

We advise that:

- We have checked the Japanese Army records, but could not find any reference to your Yoshida Akio san, however it is well known that many soldiers chose to use false names.

- Other information in your email enabled us to locate the family of the (unnamed) soldier in question.

- The family advised that their soldier passed away 15 years ago. Also, because they cannot be certain that the cap did belong to their relative; they are unwilling to receive it from you.

- Finally, the family wish to express their appreciation to your esteemed Rotary friend for looking after the cap and to you for the effort you have shown.

Noel's challenge was drawing to a close. On 19 September, though, I received a 9-page letter (in Japanese) from the daughter of the soldier, who wrote (in effect):

> Yoshida Akio san was really Yunokami Akio san and, while his given name was pronounced the same (and spelled the same in Roman letters) it was actually written with a different 'kanji'.
>
> After the war, he married and had two daughters.
>
> His wife, now 87 years old, recalled that he had worked on a farm while in Australia and had become friendly with the farmer. That said, though, we in his family did not hear a lot of details of his war experiences, even though he often talked about that time in general terms. To me, when he talked of the war, he always smiled and was never sad about things.
>
> Your details from your search confirmed for us that Yoshida Akio san was my father. He had an injured left leg and skin from his right thigh had been grafted onto it, but the skin was always stretched – it never looked normal.
>
> My mother now lives in Yonago City with me, as she is getting feeble. Our rice field at Fukumaki is leased out, but we still visit there about once a week to grow and collect vegetables.
>
> My father never really had a normal teenage life, as he was called up for army service while still young. His hobby in later life was photography and travelling within Japan. He was also a very regular attendee at reunions of his army mates, with whom he had a very close bond.
>
> We were very surprised to learn that Mr Atkins had kept the cap in such clean condition and had also tried to locate our father.
>
> We do not feel it is suitable that we now should receive the cap, but we appreciate very much yours and Mr Atkins' good will.
>
> My husband was once a fisherman and had visited Hobart on tuna boats.

It had taken just under three months to answer Noel's challenge. We sent a package to 'Yoshida san's' wife and daughter that included the cap and some brochures about Tasmania.

SCRUFFEL
Jacqueline Lonsdale Cuerton

He was just a young pup when she met him. He was new to the house but it hadn't taken long for him to establish his place in it. The superior male human wanted him to be an outside dog; the female wanted to have him inside as did the inferior male, so the smart young dog sided with the female and the boy. But this new person, a different personality altogether. The two superior beings went back to work and the boy to school, so he was left to the mercies of this female whose status he could not work out.

This female was the mother of the superior male, on a recuperative holiday after a lengthy stay in hospital. She was unsteady on her feet and did not want the dog inside. He was going to grow into a big animal and she didn't like animals inside. She didn't like pets, preferring to watch wild-life in its habitat. Dogs had uses but not inside suburban homes which were empty, usually, five days a week. She believed some had great intelligence and she admired the dogs trained for the blind, the physically disabled and some for the mentally ill.

Instinctively the young dog knew he wasn't going to win an argument with her; one foot, still midair and over the threshold didn't ever connect with the floor on the inside while she was there. He soon learned not to jump up to her when she went out and if he behaved really well, she spoke to him and tickled him behind his ears. She grew a bit stronger and kicked a ball to him. But she didn't chase after it, wrestle it back from him. He asked why, in his soft growly way, as he stood over it on the other side of the yard, daring her to 'come and get it'. She told him he had to bring it back to her, pointing to her feet.

Scruffel refused to drop it immediately in front of her; it was always about a metre away. He challenged her to take steps and felt very proud when she told him he was a clever dog. "Intuitive", she said. He heard her tell the other humans when they returned home, saying, "You know, you have a clever dog there. He could be trained to do all kinds of things."

Out of his hearing she said he was going to end up a lonely, frustrated dog. Because her son was not going to win the argument on training, discipline, he didn't try. Eventually the woman was well enough to go home. "Good -bye, Scruffel", she said, "by the time I see you again you will have forgotten everything I tried to teach you. Just be good, okay, and don't run away". Like many times before she got into the car for a trip somewhere but Scruffel knew, this time she wasn't coming back. And he was sad. She kissed his nose.

It was eight years when they met again. He'd watched a small building being erected in the big yard, furniture was installed and then, oh, joy, she arrived. But she didn't walk at all. She had a sort of motor-bike, like the man's but with four wheels and no noisy engine. She rode it into her small house and around the yard, up the street, even taking Scruffel with her. She'd throw the ball for him, all directions, trying to trick him and this time he knew he had to return the ball to her hand. He didn't even attempt to enter her little house but he could sit on the small porch and she'd talk to him from inside. She often sat at her desk working on a little machine like the ones the man and woman in the big house had. Sometimes she read something to him and she'd say, "What do you think, Scruffel, does that sound okay?" Or, "That spelling doesn't look right; how do you spell rambunctious, Scruffel? You're still rambunctious, you know; want to come for a walk with me later?" Scruffel grinned then and wagged his tail.

Soon it was noticed she was doing less, fewer walks, no ball-throwing. The man placed a chair near the sliding door leading to the porch; she would sit there and talk to Scruffel , so close, close enough to be stroked, but still outside. She was not going to break her rule.

One day she farewelled the three people in the big house and sat in her chair to read. She wasn't turning any pages though, as she usually did and Scruffel thought that was strange. In the afternoon she lay on her bed. Scruffel stood at the door softly growling, please let me in.

"All right", she said, "just one time". With his head resting on her bed she said a few words every now and then and she fondled his head and neck or just had her arm across his back. After a while she said, "You know, don't you Scruffel, I'm going?" And Scruffel made a half sob, half growl noise, his eyes so sad. She said, "We've been good friends haven't we, Scruffel, we understand each other. Be good and kind to the other people, especially the man; behave for him as you have for me. Can you do that, eh?"

She was quiet for a long time, her hand slowly stroking his back then she said, Tell him .... love .... and that was all. Her hand stopped, her eyes closed, her breathing stopped. Scruffel cried.

The afternoon wore away. Scruffel stayed, his head on the bed, her arm, heavy, on his back but he didn't want to move. The family came home, the son said he'd go to see how his mother was. He thought it was very quiet, and the dog wasn't on the porch. He looked in the door, "Mum", he said. Scruffel looked at him, a look of great sadness on his face. The son reached his mother's side in a few long strides. "Oh, Mum", he said again, sitting on the side of the bed and taking hold of her other hand.

"How long have you been here, Scruff?" His tail moved very slightly. "Did she ask you in or did you take it on yourself to keep her company?" Scruffel licked his hand and a few times licked the salt from his face."

A TICKET TO THE WORLD CUP RUGBY FINAL 1995

Ant Dry

I came across it the day before yesterday, as I was clearing out the loft; a simple picture frame, one that I had not seen in eleven years, not since we moved from Africa. The glass was still covered in Sellotape from the move. I brushed it free of dust, but when I tried to remove the Sellotape, it proved to be too old and brittle, and cracked, refusing to release its hold.

Beneath the glass I could still see, now somewhat faded, the object that had held pride of place on my office wall for many years.

It was a ticket to the 1995 Rugby World Cup Final, at Ellis Park in Johannesburg.

I've never liked Rugby. It was the school sport when I was growing up, and playing was compulsory, but I had poor ball skills, limited agility and no understanding of the game. As a player I spent my time stumbling from one scrum to the next, never really knowing or caring what happened in between.

As a spectator, I developed an amused contempt for the game. I considered the game itself to be tedious, the players to be meat heads at best, and the school's and nation's worship of it to be bewildering. After leaving school, I hoped never to have to see another game in my life. There were better things to do.

So, twenty years later when I was offered a ticket to the World Cup Rugby Final, I was in two minds. I couldn't be bothered with the game, but the ticket was offered by a prospective new customer and I wasn't sure I should turn him down.

My wife was furious and wildly jealous, complaining loudly and bitterly in public (luckily with tongue in cheek) that it should have been her and not me. That alone should have alerted me to the significance of the event.

Norman (the prospective customer) had laid on a charter flight for us. We were collected from Harare airport, flown to Johannesburg and escorted to the stadium.

I've always felt that the best parties are those you are not really expecting to enjoy. The spontaneous get together that turns into a party is always more memorable than one you have been anticipating for days.

And so it proved with this adventure.

So many years on, my memories of the day are patchy - but remain hazily suspended like a series of still photographs.

I remember standing outside the grounds before the game, absorbing the atmosphere. I could feel the tension in the air, smell the excitement. In the background the hawkers were selling souvenirs. The crowd seethed and heaved as it filtered in.

I remember the moment the South African Airways Boeing 737 flew overhead before the game. The huge plane took us all unawares, and made us all duck, as it streaked overhead with "Go Bokke" written on its undercarriage.

I remember Nelson Mandela arriving on field to greet the players and how the whole crowd leapt to their feet when they saw him, and how they took up a chant yelling, "Nelson, Nelson, Nelson" and how they roared their approval when they noticed he was wearing the teams' shirt with the captain's number written on his back.

I remember the moment South Africa kicked the winning points. It had been a pedestrian game, the sides being more cautious than adventurous. No tries had been scored, only points kicked. The winning kick came in extra time, and I remember - as if it were yesterday - standing up and yelling until my throat hurt, joyous, my arms aloft, one of over 60,000 spectators doing exactly the same thing - and the ball forever frozen between the posts.

I remember the atmosphere as we left the stadium. A sea of people all hugging themselves with joy. The air tingled with elation and crackled with excitement.

I remember the drive back to Norman's house. We took a detour through the City Centre, not normally a safe place to go. Everywhere we looked there was a party. The car hooters were blowing, the traffic was still. There was music blaring everywhere and there really, actually was dancing in the streets. Everywhere.

I remember watching in stunned amazement as a huge red necked white male, obviously by his dress a farmer from the hinterland, hugged a skinny black guy, obviously by his dress no more than a domestic worker (remember this was South Africa in 1995), and how they were both laughing and thumping each other on the back.

I remember the next morning stopping at Wimpy for breakfast on the way to the airport, and how I knew then that the whole world had changed. For the first time ever, there was no animosity between the blacks and the whites. I remember how friendly the (black) waiter was, how easy the conversation was between my (very white) host and said waiter, how we had all laughed and joked, and agreed that Mr Mandela was the greatest man on the planet, that South Africa was the greatest nation on Earth, populated by the greatest people that could be found in the universe.

I remember feeling uplifted, spiritually refreshed, emotionally enlightened as if some great truth had been revealed to me, how I felt that now all our lives were to be transformed. The whole world would be different, and indeed it was.

I remember Norman, as I left to catch the plane home, handing me my ticket and suggesting that I keep it as a memento of that day and how I told him I would take it home and frame it. And I did.

That framed ticket, had hung on the wall in my office for years, and visitors would comment on it, and I would relive that day through the telling of it, again and again, until I became confused with what was memory and what was legend.

****

So now, 23 years on there I sat, looking at my framed ticket.

How things had changed.

When we had packed up to leave Africa, I had come close to leaving my framed ticket behind. By then it had become less of an icon, and more of a symbol and constant reminder of what could have been.

It takes time, but euphoria fades and reality bites. Ingrained habits remain. Goodwill evaporates.

I stood up, took my framed ticket and did what I should have done years ago. I dropped it into the bin. As it fell, the glass shattered. The Sellotape had failed at last.

That life has gone, the memories caked in dust, broken, encrusted by Sellotape.

Time to move on.

OWED TO AN OLD GUM TREE
with a lean to the left
Allan Jamieson

I sang, *'I talk to the trees,*
but ... ' – you know the one.
I can't sing pretty.

Tree, tell me
did you like my song?
Then I heard c-c-r-r-eeak.

I'm tone deaf.
I've never been anywhere,
rooted as I am to this spot.
Tell me, what's over
the horizon?

More trees, my friend.

Great! I'm not alone after all.

Oi! You could have asked me, tree.
I live here. I'm a bird.

So, you're the one
who wakes me at dawn,
every day!

And me, your resident possum.
I'm a night owl – excuse my pun –
I can't sleep with all
your whistling and cheep-cheeping.
Bird – Go find your own tree!

Now, just a moment possum.
My nest was here before you
came in search of a bolt-hole

in my tree's trunk.

Oh, so it's *your* tree now, is it?

Taken aback by the conversation,
I ventured to sort things out.

Tree, a landlord's job
is never a happy one.
Your two squabbling tenants
are ruining the neighbourhood.
Why not sell yourself
to a logger and be made
into a house frame?
With luck, you'll find
new tenants who appreciate
a house of wood, not
dead concrete.

Do you know any loggers?

Just a minute, while
I get my axe.

ON WAKING
Meg McLaren

Sleepy head!
Gown thrown over reluctant shoulders.
Bare feet pad past the generations that line the walls.
Lives once lived and now over.
Good morning everyone,
you have protected me well.

I step into my kitchen,
toes curling on cool, polished boards,
pale light filtering through wooden blinds.
My little dog bounces and tail wags.
Races to the nearest tree and lifts a leg.
I watch as he wanders around his world,
impatient to be part of this new day.

The kitchen smells of last night's cooking.
Ripe fruit in a bowl,
the gentle hum of the refrigerator,
the morning smell of Arabian coffee.
I pull the curtains.
Across the garden to the sea,
the world drifts gently in.
Sweet jasmine trails over the balcony.
Milky stars nestle in a green sky.
Rotting seaweed, discarded by the tide,
leaves murky banks in the sand.

I stand at the window to listen to the morning news.
A careless accident,
a wood heater left burning,
a house destroyed,
a life lost.
I close my mind to the monotone
of the speaker's voice.
I am not ready for tragedy.

A seagull flies across a pewter sky
and in the distance,
a fishing boat, like a floating soul,
awaits the first catch of the day.
The sky brightens and a thin silver line
stretches along the horizon.
Dawn creeps over the silent world.

In the early morning,
my kitchen is my world,
my thoughts are my companions.
I feel at one,
Content,
I wait for the day to begin.

THINGS THAT GO BUMP IN THE NIGHT
Lesley Podmore

At this place where I live there are kangaroos that go bump in the night --- or maybe they're possums!! I haven't quite seen!

Little roos have been visiting for years. I call them "roos", although any person knowledgeable about such things will say. "Hey, they're *wallabies*". "Roos" seem to give a better impression of their is-ness, don't you think?

They come through the gate at night, hop down the path (cement), go round the corner, across the patio (cement), around another corner, along the back path (cement) and down six steps into the pocket-handkerchief space that is the back yard ---- *grass.*

I know they come regularly because of the droppings left along the way. That was a puzzle for years, (not my cat's, not dog's either) until one night, arriving home from a meeting, I spied not one but two roos outside the gate. The car pulling in sent them off in a whirl down the path, around two corners, along, and down the steps, I presume.

Now, about that bump in the night. During last spring a heat pump was fitted to this house, with its ugly metal boxy thing hung off the wall. This particular wall can only be accessed by going around *those* corners, down the steps, across some grass, and around another corner where there is a strip of lawn 8 ft. wide-ish, with one lemon tree, some currants, and foliage from many trees hanging over next-door's fence.

Since that heat pump went in there have been **bumps in the night.** The sort that occur when an animal hits the heat pump box in the dead of night.

There are crashings and bangings and even clawings, I think. This is greatly magnified because this house is sitting on a steel-framed base. Anything dropped inside it resonates as if you were all inside a drum. The mowing-man colliding with *that box* has the same effect.

So, many nights I've been woken by crashings and bangings and clawings!! I think -- "Maybe it's not roos. Could be possums!!" They eat my lemons --- nibble the skin and leave the rest!! They have a nest in one of next-door's trees. Now that makes sense. "The little buggers are climbing all over it," I think. If they had ideas of getting into the roof space they've not managed it yet. And anyway it would be far simpler to leap from their tree.

"Why don't I go and look?" you say. Well I have got the torch, the sort that lights up like a laser and causes damage to eyes --- (a present from my son). That's simple getting the torch. The next bit involves pulling up the blind in my bedroom --- noisy --- raising the window ---- equally as noisy --- poking my head right out, and shining the torch. Well, they've long gone!!

So the annoyance remains.

You might say "Why don't you just shut that gate?" Well there is a reason involving a gate that's been hung cack-handed and a finger that has a dead nerve-damaged bit on the tip just where it connects with my harp strings when playing ---- but that's another story altogether.

ODE TO A GREY SHRIKE-THRUSH
(*Colluricincla Harmonica*)
Lelsey Podmore – Dec. 2016

Thou piper of tunes in the clear light of day,
Thou sleek little bird with feathers of grey,
You make my heart sing when you come near to me
And call in full tune ---- Duke Willee --- Duke Willee.

You come as a herald from worlds in the sky,
The angels are saying "Peace, do not cry",
They even are saying "Joy comes with this bird,
He pipes divine blessings for all, to be heard".

Duke Willee ---- Duke Willee ---- Duke Willee – ee

TOO MUCH RAIN
Jennie Herrera

Clouds riven, late sun catching
Bare branches.
Rain drops, lustre-bright,
Neatly spaced.
People in the space that's self;
People neatly ranged about the fire,
Charged with intimations.
Conversing.
A question tossed around the semi-circle:
What is God's greatest gift?
I never say God, says one, but gift, hmmm …
This, another says, friends gathered,
While it storms outside.
A sense of sharing, offered,
But fearing the sound of sentiment.
The senses, a man says.
Someone rises, throws on another log,
Pokes up a stream of sparks.
Beauty, he adds. Fun. Laughter. Hope and
Kindness. The way they overlap and underlie.
No, says an older woman.
The greatest gift is Evil.
The lightness of this time evaporates,
Leaves a sense of combat.
We can do without evil, we've got
Anger, doubt, frustration,
Boredom, folly—isn't that enough?
But—don't you see?
Good without Evil is meaningless.
Those things are Evil gathering up
Its troops, hardening into place,
Preparing for the ultimate.
She rises swiftly,
Goes to the window.
See the rain along the bough?

Each drop neat and hung apart.
Let the sun go in, more rain fall,
Each drop will gather till its weight
Makes it fall, tells us what it is.
Good feeds on little things:
A moment of kindness,
A generous thought. Tenderness.
She pulls the curtains closed.
Blots out a luminescent dusk.
Feed things. They grow. Starve them.
Saintly forbearance, someone nods,
If there was nothing to forbear—
The fire spits; wet wood sizzling.
—no saints, no vision of a better world.
And in reaching—each step takes us closer …
But it's easy here, warm, well-fed, content.
They look around the room.
Yes, it's easy, sitting here,
To talk of Evil. A concept, not a presence.
But, don't you see, she warms her hands,
Evil makes us choose, drives us forward,
Shows us; heightens each sense,
Each step, makes us *choose*.
'Resist not evil'? And what of promises
Of victory: good over evil, final nirvana;
Repentance? They look above the mantel;
The figure with its lantern.
When God has won hasn't meaning lost its meaning?
In your theory.
Grown, certainly, in love and wisdom.
But back where you began. A deeper sense of good,
I grant, when you love your enemies;
A grander concept of living life but still …
No, she gropes, 'you too can be perfect'
We dismiss too easily, say 'that's not us' …
But perfect is the moment when we cease
To behave, we cease to need to choose,
We *know* … we've touched God,
Good and Evil cease to war within us,

Because we simply are,
We've become a part of eternal love,
Not struggling with the idea, the hope,
The comfort, the belief …
She looked into the glowing caverns of the fire,
New rain beat against the roof.
We've come home.
The others who'd been honing arguments
Feel something gather,
Relieve them of a need
To lose those lustrous fattened drops
Upon the rocks below the bough.

EVENTS FROM MY WORKING LIFE
Allan Jamieson

Ah, yes ... I remember...

Chemical Engineering students were required to undertake summer vacation work relevant to their course. At the end of my first year at Uni. (1958), I signed up for three months' work as a Fitter's Mate at a large chemical processing plant in Melbourne. It was my task to carry the tools for the Fitter and to do things for his amusement – such as go to the store and ask for a Long Weight. After standing at the counter for quite a while, I learned that it was actually "a long wait".

I was there really to experience maintenance work and I learned a lot! For instance, many design engineers never think that equipment or machines will ever *need* repairing! Engineers can design factories *without* the Fitter's needs in mind.

In a chemical factory, there are many tanks in which chemicals are stored or blended. A typical tank has a slightly conical bottom – with the low point at the centre, from where a pipe runs to the inlet of a pump – and the whole tank is raised above the ground by four or six legs to allow room for the pump to be placed underneath. That's fine, but pumps have glands that provide a seal to stop any liquid in the pump from leaking along the drive shaft from the motor and onto the ground. Pump glands eventually leak and need to be replaced. The legs of the tank are never long enough so that the Fitter could walk underneath the tank. The Fitter cannot even sit under the tank! No, he has to crawl or slide on his belly to get to the gland and work while lying on his back or on his side and all the while his clothes get wet from whatever chemical was leaking.

Five years later, after graduating from university, I worked briefly at the Sydney factory of that same company, where a new process plant had been installed based on a design done by engineers at the Melbourne factory. For construction purposes, an engineer had drawn a side-view ('elevation') of the main reaction tank; this showed the positions of the only two openings required in the vertical sides of the tank to cater for external fittings – a thermocouple probe and a screw feeder. The tank had then been manufactured exactly to that drawing; as a consequence, the thermocouple opening had been positioned directly *under* the screw feeder.

Now, it transpired that the thermocouple probes didn't last long and they had to be drawn out frequently and replaced. What should have been a ten-minute task was, instead, a three-hour job, because before we could pull out the probe, we first had to dismantle the screw feeder from the tank and its motor – a heavy lift job – and, of course, this equipment had to be reconnected and carefully aligned again before the plant could be restarted.

A major design error! The probe could have been located anywhere around the circumference of the tank: moving it even 20 centimetres to left or right of where it was actually installed would have meant the probe would 'clear' the screw feeder when pulled out. That design engineer did not think of the repair needs, *and* to show this improved probe location, he would have had to prepare a second drawing, so we can conclude that he was also lazy!

Back in that factory in Melbourne, in the basement of one of the chemical plants, maintenance workers operated a laundry, a hairdressing salon and an (illegal) SP bookmaking office – all on behalf of themselves and fellow employees, not for the company. I noticed that things changed at about 4:00 pm every day when the engineers would come down the stairs seeking 'volunteers' to stay back on overtime to complete necessary maintenance jobs. Of course, this work could have (and should have) been done during the day but the workers would earn more if it *"had to be done"* on overtime. The workers and the engineers both understood tacitly that – to get any maintenance work done at all – the workers would be allowed to laze away their time in the basement until the clock moved around to when overtime had to be paid.

Why would management put up with this? You only need to ask the trade unions to which the maintenance workers belonged – *Industrial blackmail!*

That new process plant in Sydney had a long commissioning period and – at one point – I worked six weeks continuous night shift without a break. Ever since, whenever an opportunity has arisen to work shifts, I have always volunteered for the night shift and pushed others to do likewise.

Why? Because it is the best time to learn how a piece of machinery or a process should work. On day shift, there is always a manager ("hard hat") around who wants to change something. Chaos usually rules. When the afternoon shift operator arrives, the coterie of interfering managers slowly diminishes and near the end of that shift, the operator finally has a chance to set all the controls in their right place – in effect, to return to how it <u>should</u> operate.

The night shift operator then has an easy task, except that if something does go wrong, he has to solve the problem himself. On day shift, there are always a dozen "experts" around and he can ask for their advice, but on night shift *"the buck stops here"* is the reality; there is no better way to understand how things work than to have to fix them yourself. As an engineer, I felt that this opportunity is vital: If you do not learn something new every day, then you are wasting your time!

Ah, yes …. I remember ….

===//===

The best laid plans

The world's first oxygen pulp bleaching stage started up in 1970 at a large pulp mill in northern Sweden. Soon processing 150 tonnes of pulp per day, it was nonetheless a *pilot plant* and the three project leaders – of whom I was one – had a long list of trials and tests to run over the next two years. Bengt, the project leader representing the equipment design company, had one item near the top of his list: "Rupture Discs."

The oxygen stage was unique in the pulp industry, comprising a tall, cylindrical gas-filled pressure vessel with oxygen being the gas. Yet, it also would have a large column of fluffed, semi-dry pulp inside. A conventional safety valve, similar to one that would be serviceable on a boiler, might soon plug with pulp if installed on an oxygen "reactor" (it was not a "tower" to us pioneer experimenters) so this pilot reactor was equipped with two rupture discs near the top. If one disc blew, would a reaction force arise that could topple the reactor over, if the legs did not provide adequate resistance to this force? Would the vent tube stay clear, unblocked by pulp? What else might happen? There was nothing even remotely like this equipment anywhere else in the world.

Bengt was an Electrical Engineer – if electrical engineers are not thorough in planning their work, they are soon dead! Bengt's plan was to put a fluffed pulp column inside the reactor, attach strain gauges to the legs, then pressurise the vessel with nitrogen until a disc ruptured. The test was managed from the control room. A team of observers was stationed on the ground and one of their tasks was to warn passers-by that a test was underway: *"Please move on promptly"* was to be the message. We did not want spectators, as we weren't sure what might happen. The roadway could not be cordoned off.

Sture and Allan: Oxygen reactor in background. One rupture disc can be seen where the men are working.

Shift change was at 6:00 am and Bengt had calculated that the disc would rupture at about 11:00 am when traffic in the area would be at its minimum. Unfortunately, the liquid nitrogen vaporizer was undersized and was soon covered in ice. In the control room, we could only settle down to watch the pressure gauge move ever so slowly upward.

The observers on the ground outside began their task diligently; as expected, the traffic flow lessened and their attention to duty lessened too – 11:00 am came and went – nothing happened. 12 noon came and the observers wandered off to get a bite to eat. When the disc did blow, at 2:00 pm, there wasn't an observer in sight, but it was now shift change time and the traffic flow was again at a peak.

In the control room, the experiment was a success. Bengt could analyse the instrument records there. What about outside? There was more than 20 tonne of fluffed pulp all over the roadway but nobody in sight. The pulp mill's project leader, Sture, rang the first-aid centre, the gatehouse and the foreman's office but there were no reports of injuries. We had been lucky, it seemed.

The next morning though, a foreman rang: A worker wanted to speak to Sture. Somewhat nervous, Sture went to meet the fellow. Their conversation:

Sture: *"Tell me what happened."*

Man: *"Well, I was on me bike on the way home. Me mind was on other things. Then, there was this almighty BANG above me and I was blown off the bike."*

Sture: *"Do you have any injuries?"*

Man: *"Me legs are sore."* Sture's heart missed a beat, but then the man lent forward close to Sture and said: *"You know, I'd really love to know how fast I ran the first 100 metres!"* The two laughed.

The experiment had gone well!

===//===

A Modern-Day Viking

In the 1970's when I worked at that pulp mill in northern Sweden, there were two pulp lines. The pine line came first and had been expanded many times over the years. There were three bleaching sequences for pine and about 22 drum washers inside on the third floor of the bleach plant building.

Göte had been Production Manager of the mill for many years. With good reason! Nobody, anywhere, could have been more production-orientated than Göte (pronounced YUR-TE). As an example of Göte's determination, it was said that any washer could be connected to any other washer so that – if a wire filter mesh came off one washer – production could continue, because another washer could be brought into use. It was certainly true that only Göte knew how to do this through the maze of pipes that ran horizontally under the washer floor and up and down to the ground floor. "Wooden welds" were a very visible feature of these pipes: Whenever a hole arose in a pipe and the leak became noticeable a cone of wood would be hammered into the hole. Some "welds" were years old, simply being hammered further in if the metal of the pipe continued to corrode. The piping network resembled elongated porcupines.

It was the other production line, however, that I want to tell you about. In the late 1960's, a 900 tonne per day birch pulp mill was built. The bleach line had five up-flow towers and these were installed side-by-side in a line along the outer wall of the building that housed the pine bleachery. Being just 350 km south of the Arctic Circle, the winters are cold (average year-round temperature is 0°C with a winter low of around minus 35°C) so the bottom portions of the towers were enclosed in one new elongated building to keep the thick stock pumps, tower mixers, *etc*. "inside"].

At about 2:00 am one night, Göte's phone woke him at home: The pulp inlet pipe at the bottom of one tower had ruptured. The tower had emptied and its contents of close-on 1,800 tonnes of pulp and water now filled the extra building to its roof. Such an event had not been planned for by the design engineers; the access to the building was by man-sized doors only. How to get the pulp out?

At about 4:00 am, a loud explosion woke the people in the nearby town. Göte had rung a fisherman friend of his and together they went down to the mill. Göte knew that his friend routinely used dynamite – that marvellous invention of the Swede, Alfred Nobel – to catch fish. At the bleach plant, Göte asked: *"Could you knock a hole in the wall here big enough for a front-end loader to go through?"* The man set too and the result was a success. By 4:30 am, the bricks and rubble had been cleared away and the loader was moving around inside the building.

Yes indeed! Göte was a modern-day Viking.

OLD SPY WANTS TO COME HOME
Jennie Herrera

Small item in newspapers:

Raymond Krill, suspected of spying for the Soviet Union in the 1950s and 1960s, says he would like to come home. For the past three decades Krill, 81, has lived in Prague. Although never charged with espionage his precipitous departure from Australia in December 1969 was taken by many people as proof of his guilt.

*

I can't think why every interview televised with him, every photo snapped, shows him standing smack-bang in front of a 'postcard'. There he is, still looking as seamed and tough as ever, in front of Prague Castle, in the centre of Wenceslas Square, on the Charles Bridge with mute swans fortuitously caught in the picture. It is as though he stood just where the cameras could pan *so-o-o* beautifully. I wonder if the Czech Tourist Bureau set it up? Because old spies lurk in anonymous tenements (can you imagine Philby standing in front of the Kremlin—oh look, folks, here I am), they melt into the dullness of concrete office blocks, they lurk in look-alike reaches of suburbia …

*

Overheard conversation at a Canberra party:

"So Krill has finally confessed?"

"Only guilt by suggestion, they've never actually linked him to the mysterious K that came up with the Petrovs—"

"I thought they were sure K was Clayton?"

"They weren't sure of *anything*, dear boy. If ever there was a failure as a source it was Petrov … I've always been inclined to think he defected because he didn't want to go home and show how meagre his pickings had been—"

"Well, except for the British bomb tests and all the business over the Communist Party it's hard to see exactly what there *was* to pick."

"I suppose a good spy highlights his material … but we're looking at it from the wrong end. We really only know what Petrov told the Royal Commission and he never mentioned Krill—"

"But isn't that the point? When Krill went everyone assumed he'd been a sleeper all those years, briefly activated, then pulled out."

"So—the late sixties—what was he highlighting then? Vietnam, I suppose."

*

The papers sound remarkably definite, don't they? So certain Raymond *does* want to come home after all this time. But no one has caught him actually saying so. But then he never did say much. Wild horses, my mother used to say … but he could say a lot without words, just that kind of comfortable bulkiness, that sense of rock-solid being, he was a very *safe* person. And he hasn't changed. The interviewers do the talking, he stands there and looks into the camera, and it's impossible to guess what he's thinking. But I wouldn't be in the least surprised if it's "I'll let this little twerp rabbit on for awhile." Then, as soon as the camera ceases to roll, no doubt he'll say something like, "fancy a cup of something hot—and you can tell me how is life down under, these days," and out of that the young reporter will try to weave a dramatic story.

*

Excerpt from a long article in a daily newspaper:

Raymond Krill was never linked to any particular party and definitely not the CPA. The only thing that ever suggested a bias was his alleged statement "You don't ban them, you keep them in the public eye and know what's going on." He was known to be a very private man, taciturn, expressionless, "wooden" was a popular adjective among his colleagues, but competent. His family life was lived outside the hot-house of Fifties Canberra. But one person who remembers him well said he had a habit, in the rare times he came to a party or barbecue, of arriving very late. He would excuse his tardiness as the result of trouble with his car. At the time no one thought anything of it but after his defection it was suggested he timed his arrival to coincide with the period when people had been drinking awhile but before they were likely to start leaving.

*

I was devastated when he went because he went alone. He always said it was only for awhile, then we'd see each other again. But the months passed, turned into years, nothing was said … and of course I was of an age when simply sitting round and waiting never occurred to me …

But the gulf, the gap, the hole, I'm not sure what to call it, in my youthful psyche was real and deep and lasting. I filled it with *activities*, anything really. I'm not sure I could claim, now, that I suffered any lasting psychological damage. But it made me wary. The rock-solid can crumble. Love can depart, not totally, but to a distance from which it is hard to believe its assertions any more.

*

Discussion by the production team of a current affairs program:

"Can we link it to something on the Petrovs, the referendum on the Communist Party … maybe the decision to go into Vietnam?"

"The trouble is—and I've checked every report on Krill—you'd have to have an interview with him as the centerpiece, the hook to hang it on—and he just doesn't *talk*, every single item puts words in his mouth. That might do for two minutes but not for an hour."

"Then why not make the Petrovs the story and him the icing?"

"Mmm, you could have 'What Happened to the Petrovs?' Didn't he end up working in a factory in Melbourne?"

"They're both dead now, surely?"

"Yes, she died only the other day and he went some years back. But you'd have to call the program 'Who *Were* the Petrovs?' Half our viewers were barely born then."

"Despite what they say about the ageing population? Wasn't there a jingle about her, I think her name was Evdokia, which got turned into Eve the temptress. It started off 'Vladimir delved and Eve span, Then the Call went out and the Petrovs ran—' Something like that—"

"That's even worse than the one about Profumo … you know, 'Half a pound of Mandy Rice, half a pound of Keeler, Mix 'em up and what've you got? A bloody sexy sheila!' But back to Krill … it's all very vague and I doubt our budget will stretch to Prague, so can we find someone here who really *knows* something and is willing to talk?"

*

Raymond treated Australia as though it had ceased to exist, just an address on an envelope—and those got opened and read for years after he went. Then they seemed to lose interest though I'm not sure any suspect is ever totally wiped off their books, that isn't how they work. Blot your copybook and the Head never lets you out of his sights. And they knew he knew Ian Milner in Prague. They were convinced Milner was a Soviet spy. Guilt by association. Nor was it just that he *knew* Milner but that he genuinely *liked* him. But I'm not sure that he was a good judge of people …

*

Excerpt from a weekly column:

The wife of a retired cabinet minister says she remembers Krill. "In those days my husband hated it if there was a do at the Russian Embassy he could not avoid. He used to call their functions 'the gorilla games', because he said they were all uncultured, uneducated, hairy, and had peculiar teeth! But I don't remember ever seeing Raymond there.

"It was said Krill was a corruption of Kroll and that the family was German several generations back. But it didn't seem to matter. That was over and done with and a new page turned. No, it was people who had 'ov' or 'ski' at the end of their names who got us worried. I'm not surprised Lionel Murphy's wife changed her name. I would too if I'd been born a Grzonkowski.

"In the days when men were expected to be strong and silent and bronzed, their eyes fixed on the far horizon, Raymond was strong and silent to a tee. You hardly ever got a word out of him. There was something about him which suggested a settled fact. Yet he was so still it was almost uncanny. You never felt his emotions, he had no sex appeal, he didn't even wear aftershave to let something linger. Though I remember he always dressed neatly, almost stylishly. The ties men wore in those days! I think they closed their eyes and stabbed.

"He was a big man, six feet or more, and quite burly. Even so, he had this extraordinary capacity to melt into the crowd. It must have been useful if he really *was* memorising all our conversations!"

*

We always met in Cologne or Amsterdam—and in churches. We would sit in a back pew, just sit, talking quietly, sometimes for an hour or more. Then, if no one was showing any interest, we'd go to a restaurant or walk together in the narrow streets. Is this the message in the photos of Prague. Remember then, those wonderful medieval churches still standing despite wars and upheavals and centuries ... people do survive. They survive the sense of betrayal. They come back. They regroup. They find hope in the strangest places.

I'm surprised the media hasn't come calling. I asked the nurses to imply that I am going senile. It goes against the grain. A wheelchair, yes, but my mind is still bright and sharp. My memory of that fateful year is still crisp and ... I am tempted to say complete but I wonder if that is so. Many *many* things I have since wondered about. And I am not sure I will ever know the answers. Perhaps that is the true meaning of 'the human condition', that partial window overlooking the complete.

*

A spokesman for the Minister for Immigration:

Mr Raymond Krill has not applied for a visa to visit Australia. Nor has he had any contact with our Embassy. We understand his Australian passport expired a number of years ago after three renewals in West Germany and Ghana. We believe he now travels on a German passport. If and when Mr Krill applies for an Australian visa, his situation will be reviewed.

*

The irony is—he always had German citizenship. He went through World War II, spending two years in New Guinea, and no one ever asked. He received the D.S.O. and several lesser gongs. So I suppose, if they'd asked later, they would've been prepared to overlook it ... And his mother being Dutch gave the suggestion that Krill was, well, something of that nature. His father stayed in Dutch New Guinea. That added to the assumption. It proved a good background when, postwar, he faded back into anonymity. If he'd been a member of a Union ... or if he'd associated with members of what they now say was definitely a conspiracy, 'the nest of traitors', names, faces, jobs, motivations, all firmly linked to the KGB ... But he didn't 'associate'; that was his protection and his tragedy.

If he could've talked things over with sympathetic people, found a resonance in other people's beliefs, shared a sympathetic insight. Instead he bottled it up—till it burst the bounds and he couldn't look anyone, not colleagues, not politicians, not anyone, in the face.

Their faces, he says in the photocopy he gave me of his 'ground zero' diary, were complacent smug faces. White faces. Fat faces. Greedy faces. I'm not sure why he concentrated so much on faces. Did he believe he could read expressions but couldn't read minds …

If he came back now, would he feel we have changed, that we have extended our boundaries of sympathy, that we can see the pain in a brown face as clearly as we can see anguish in blue eyes and red lips. I'm not sure …

*

Excerpts from a left-wing newsletter titled 'Was he one of us—or one of them?'

Even now, thirty-three years after Raymond Krill left Australian shores for Prague, never to return, there are doubts as to whether ASIO believed he was KGB or whether he was sent to Prague to ferret for our Secret Service. And the goons aren't telling … After the war he entered External Affairs as a cadet and rose slowly through the ranks. He made a visit to Port Moresby in 1965 reportedly in response to criticisms levelled at the slow pace of Australia's preparation for PNG independence. Krill's Department files were gathered in by the spooks at the time of his sudden departure and they remain classified. So we wait for some public-spirited person to leak them.

*

He always said touching down in Port Moresby was a kind of 'coming home', though he didn't find it an attractive town and avoided the company of expatriate Australians. They walked freely, he felt, where his grandfather had been denied. This suggests a deep sense of family which his own actions contradict. Yet he *did* care deeply about family, both on a detached level, family as concept, and on a personal level. He denied himself, squirrelled away funds in an account in his mother's name. No matter what his choices were he didn't want anyone related to him to ever have to go cap-in-hand …

*

Interview with a senior member of the Canberra Press Gallery:

Q. What is your take on the resurrection of the 'Krill Affair'? You knew him quite well—

A. I don't know about 'quite well'. Raymond Krill kept his own counsel. But one curious thing I've noticed is there has been very little attention paid to his links to New Guinea. His grandfather was the owner of a copra plantation taken over without compensation after WWI. He took the family to Hollandia where he worked for the Dutch. His son wrote a book on 'cargo cults' and sent his wife and children to Brisbane in the 1930s, ostensibly for their education and, possibly, to find a publisher for his book. But the War intervened, young Raymond left school, joined the AIF, and went back to New Guinea. It was said he went into Dutch New Guinea as an agent for us but, so far, I haven't been able to confirm this.

Q. What about the book? Was it ever published?

A. It seems not. His wife was asked about it before she died. She said she believed the publisher lost the manuscript. Does happen. But it helped keep tongues wagging …

*

Raymond was furious that a manuscript on which his father had lavished ten years and dozens of unique photographs could be so casually mislaid. But I suppose it was nothing to his father's sense of misery and betrayal in 1962 when he realised the Dutch were going to walk away from their responsibilities. He could never *bear* to hear the story of Pontius Pilate in church, not that he was a regular churchgoer … though he never quite lost his faith …

*

Draft for a sermon by an elderly Canberra cleric:

Raymond Krill was a man you could rely on. As a young minister in Fifties Canberra when everything looked so disturbingly *unfinished* I was keen to plant some trees round the church. Next Saturday Raymond turned up, armed with a spade and mattock, and lo-and-behold we had our trees.

It was said he was unpunctual about work but I suspect this had to do with a growing sense of disillusionment. He told me it was not the cultural cringe that defined us but an unassailable belief that we were decent folk ruled by decent folk. It was a form of corruption that we could not take any criticism that might challenge this view. When a non-Australian and a black African to boot dared criticise aspects of Australia's administration of New Guinea it created *outrage* behind closed Department doors … *we knew what was best for our natives* … But it was when the Department asked him to make sure refugees from west of the border could not pass through our territory to reach New York, before the UN voted … He came to me and said 'Padre, hand me that bowl of water … ' Six months later, I received a letter from Prague. He wrote, 'I came to bathe in the puddles of the Prague 'spring', to rub shoulders with people who understand what betrayal really means' …

*

I understand the message: 'You see me testing the waters. I love Prague but if you need me I will come.' Of course I can say, yes, come, now that I can no longer come to you … but you are too frail and I am too crippled … and I forgave you long ago, Dad … and I still get a kind of secret satisfaction from the thought of ASIO having to pore through every letter and memo you ever wrote, every damning note in your margins …

SCABBY
Ant Dry

<u>Burnie, Australia 2015</u>

Simon walked up isle thirteen as directed. Canned tomatoes would be on the right, the shelf packer had said. He looked at the array of products. No cans of tomatoes leapt out and bit him on the nose. Where the bloody hell were they? God, this was frustrating. Baked beans, peas, asparagus, green beans, artichokes. No tomatoes.

He looked around in frustration. There was another shelf packer, busy about twenty meters away. He walked over.

'Excuse me. Where are the tinned tomatoes?'

The packer turned around and Simon recoiled in shock.

It couldn't be. It must be thirty years. Simon felt himself shift to a different time, a whole continent away.

"Scabby?" he asked.

******

<u>The Matibi Tribal Trust Land – Rhodesia 1978</u>

The combat stick had been on foot patrol for about five days. Simon had been trudging along with his mind in neutral, looking forward to the next break and a nice mug of tea, when Scabby the stick leader had started yelling.

'CONTACT CONTACT CONTACT'

By pure instinct, Simon dived for cover, looking up to see where Scabby was, cursing himself for his lack of vigilance.

Scabby was on his knees behind a rock firing towards the river. Simon looked toward the river and could see nothing. He squeezed off a shot anyway, hoping to see something, anything.

Scabby was hysterical with excitement.

'FIRE AT WILL, FIRE AT WILL' he screamed, following his own lead.

Simon fired off a few more rounds and then yelled,

'Where are they?'

'Jesus fucking Christ, are you fucking blind?' Scabby was enraged. He looked at the rest of the stick. 'Who saw the gooks?'

Simon shrugged, and looked at Smithy and Alan, who looked bewildered.

'There's nothing there, Scabs.' Said Smithy

'Yeah, I didn't see anything either.' Alan admitted.

Munyaradzi, the black interpreter, stood mute.

Scabby emptied the rest of his magazine in the direction of the river.

'I tell you they were there.' He muttered darkly.

The radio, strapped to Scabby's back, crackled into life.

'Delta Tango three confirm you have contact?'

Scabby's eyes widened. He reached for the mouthpiece

'Ah roger, relay one we have an unconfirmed sighting. We are going in to investigate.' He turned to his team.

'Come on you wankers. We're gonna find those gooks. Follow me.'

Now on full alert, Simon followed Scabby, with Alan Munyaradzi and Smithy behind.

They made very slow progress until they arrived at the river.

'There's a village on the other side,' whispered Scabby, we're going in.

The "river" was really only a dry sandy river bed, so in no time at all they arrived at the village, a sad little collection of round mud huts, their thatch badly in need of repair. A completely naked child and a very old man were the only inhabitants. The child played in the dust with a stick and the old man slept. A fire in the middle of the kraal smoked slowly, needing attention. A battered old kettle stood next to it.

All was peaceful.

Simon, Smithy and Alan took up positions at the edge of the kraal, defensively facing outwards.

'Munyaradzi, come with me.' Scabby walked into the middle of the kraal. The child looked up, saw the white man and bolted.

Scabby walked up to the fire, and kicked the kettle viciously, aiming at the slumbering old man. The old man leapt to his feet to avoid the flying metal and stream of boiling water.

Scabby laughed loudly. 'You lazy old shit, I knew you wouldn't be sleeping through all that noise. Munyaradzi, ask him where the gooks are.'

There was some chatter in the vernacular.

Munyaradzi looked relieved. 'The old man, he say they gandangas have never been here. He will not allow them in this village.

He is a friend of the government.'

Scabby laughed. 'Bullshit.' He said. 'Tell the stupid fucker I shall burn his village down if he doesn't tell me where the gooks are.'

Munyaradzi looked crestfallen. He turned back to the old man. More chatter, lots of gesticulating. Arms flapped, hands waved.

'Enough of this bullshit. What does he say?'

Munyaradzi looked apologetic.

'He say there are no gandangas.'

Simon looked over his shoulder to see what was going on. He watched as Scabby smiled, lifted his boot and kicked the old man in the head. The old man's head snapped back. His emaciated body flew backwards, bounced and came to a rest next to the fire.

Munyaradzi, looking like a deer frozen in a truck's headlights, started to sway on his feet.

Simon stepped into the village. 'Fuck's sake Scabby, you stupid prick, what have you done?'

Scabby turned on him his rifle raised pointing directly at Simon.

'Who's a stupid prick, you fucking little wanker? Call me that again, and I'll fucking shoot you dead.'

Simon swallowed.

Smithy came to stand next to Simon. 'Calm down Scabby.'

'CALM DOWN. JESUS CHRIST WHO ARE YOU WANKERS? THERE ARE FUCKING GOOKS ALL AROUND US AND YOU WANT ME TO CALM DOWN. THIS LITTLE SHIT KNOWS WHERE THE GOOKS ARE. I'M INTERROGATING HIM.'

Scabby was panting and his rifle moved between Simon and Smithy.

'Okay, okay, everything's quite fine. Just put down your weapon,' said Simon gently moving his hand towards the barrel and slowly moving it away from his face.

'Alan, you better have a look at the old man.' Alan was the medic. He didn't know much more than Simon, but he had at least had some first aid training.

Keeping his eye on Scabby, Alan bent over the old man, feeling his neck.

'Shit, Simon, he's dead.'

'He was harbouring terrorists' said Scabby suddenly sounding very defensive.

Simon sighed.

Looking at each other, the stick knew that this was just the beginning of the affair.

******

Burnie Australia 2015

Scabby, squatting in isle thirteen in Woolies, looked up and squinted.

'What?' he asked

'Um. Tomatoes?' mumbled Simon. There was no question about it, the accent hadn't changed, the vocal inflection was the same. The eyes were identical.

'Scabby? It's Simon. Matibi Tribal Trust Land? 1978? Remember?'

Scabby's eyes narrowed.

'Maybe. Tomatoes are over there.' And he flicked his hand languidly.

Hesitantly Simon held out his hand.

'How you doing? I didn't know you were in Oz. How long have you been here?'

Scabby ignored the outstretched hand. His eyes dropped and he shuffled his feet.

A young woman, just out of her teens and dressed in the Woolies uniform appeared over Scabby's shoulder.

'Do you need any assistance?' she asked of Simon.

Scabby stood looking dejected.

'Ah, no, I was just asking directions.'

The woman turned to Scabby.

'I've told you before' she said, as if addressing a four year old. 'Don't just stand there looking stupid. Help the customer. Show the gentleman what he wants and then get back to your packing. I don't want to keep telling you the same thing. You know you're on your last warning already. Don't let me have to speak to you again.'

'I'm sorry Jeanette' mumbled Scabby, not looking up from his feet.

Simon felt his ears turn red.

'I've got what I need, thanks,' he mumbled.

'Oh, good' said Jeanette, 'I'll let you get along then' and she stalked off.

Simon turned back to Scabby, but Scabby had departed, scurrying off with an empty carton under his arm. As he arrived at the end of the isle, he turned and looked back at Simon. Their eyes met. Scabby shrugged lightly, lifted his hand in a half-hearted wave, and disappeared.

WOUNDS
Dawn Meredith

"Oh, it's nothing," he said, as the blood dripped down the side of his craggy nose. "Was just a little careless in the garden, that's all."

"But Dad," I insisted, touching the top of his bald, sun-spotted head with one fingertip, "You should see a doctor." I looked around at the cramped space that was now my father's world. A single living room, with french doors overlooking a nicely tended garden. His home was crowded with overstuffed armchairs, bookcases, a giant telly and his marital bed, which he had refused to part with no matter what the Director said in her patient, 'I'm tolerating you because you're a new resident and your daughter is standing right beside me' voice.

"I'm fine." He waved me away and sat down with wobbly dignity. I bit my lip watching him, the man who used to swing up in his sinewy arms and hurl me round and round until I screamed in delight-fright. Was it time to make one of those things I heard about on the radio this morning – an 'End of Life Plan'?

"I'll just get a flannel," I said, going to the bathroom, designed especially for wheelchairs. Returning with a cold, damp cloth I dabbed his splotchy head. The blood was drying.

"I know what you're thinking," he said. "That since Mum died I can't look after myself. That I'm a tottery old fool."

"No…" I said half-heartedly. *Yes,* I thought. He looked up at me then, with his brilliant gem-cut blue eyes. "I'm still your dad, you know. Still the guy you used to argue with, who chased you around the yard." He chuckled. "Cracked a shot into the loungeroom window, remember?"

I nodded. It was one of Dad's favourite stories. All I remembered was Mum's fury. We couldn't afford to replace the glass on such a huge window. Dad was reckless, silly, childlike, in Mum's mind. I sighed. And yet they had such a happy marriage overall. My face felt hot and I turned away. Ten years without her and it still hurt like hell. I felt his hand on my arm.

"Pet, it's OK to cry," he said in a gravelly voice. I turned to him. I wanted to dive into his lap and snuggle there but he looked so frail, with the blood and all. And his arms were rigid and thin these days. I might break something. Where was the comfort in your parents getting old? Where was I supposed to turn when my dad was gone? "Sit," he said, pointing to the chair beside me. "I might not be able to fit you on my lap anymore, but I'm still here for you." The blood was dried and dark now. I scrubbed a little harder on the side of his face and laughed, despite my tears.

"You haven't lost your marbles yet, then," I said.

"You'll know when the time is right," he said quietly, watching me.

"Right for what?" I said, evading the truth, holding the flannel in the air.

"Time to take over. You know."

"Dad…"

"It's all part of the master plan, Pet. It's the natural order of things. I cared for you, now you care for me."

"I wish it were that simple," I said bitterly.

"It is if you let go," he replied.

"Of what?" I felt the anger rise, the injustice of losing your parent to DEATH, that cheat, that hated enemy.

"Of the need to be nourished and comforted."

"But how can anyone live without that?" I blurted angrily, rising to my feet. I stormed over to the window. The sundrenched garden stared back with flower bonneted faces, elegant tree limbs reached towards me, soft grass beckoned me to lie there in the shade.

"There's comfort everywhere," he said from his seat behind me. "You just have to look."

I blinked back the tears and wiped my nose noisily.

"I don't know if I can," I whispered.

Dad, his hearing perfect even now, heard me.

"You will. You'll find the strength to do amazing things. Trust me. Just like a teabag. You don't know how…"

"…strong you are until you're put in hot water." I finished for him. It was a favourite saying of Mum's. I turned and smiled at him. "Sorry. I came to see how you were, not to depress you."

He reached out his hand and I took hold of it. It was warm and big and strong.

"I'll always be here for you," he said, "Even when I'm not." I looked at him quizzically. He pointed at his bedside drawer. "Been waiting for the right time to give it to you and I think it's today."

"What?" I said, opening the drawer. There was the usual old person stuff, medications, hankies, etc. And a large fat leather note-book. I lifted it out. "Is this it?" He nodded. I closed the drawer and sat down again, handing it over. He took it, held it close to his face and breathed in slowly. Then, his eyes shining, he handed it back to me.

"Yours now."

I opened it slowly, feeling the years in the weight of it, all the words, hand written in his flowing script. And there was the first line: *On this day, April 9th, 1966, my beautiful daughter Helen was born. She is the most stunning, intricate, loveable thing I have ever seen.*

A TOUCH OF CARPE DIEM
Ant Dry

I'm not old but well aware
That time is passing by
The endless flame which still blows hot
Will soon begin to flag
It will flicker, and it will fade
Till snuffed by reach of time
I'd hate to think that I'd be sit
Upon my little cloud
With harp in hand and grapes beside
With frets that life had flown.
Sinatra sings of few regrets
I'd love to say the same.
But who of us can really tell
Of lives fulfilled and fine?
How many of us can say with fair
They leave no guilt behind?
So let's begin a new life now
With plans to live not die
A life with love and pain unknown
With ne' the sound of a cry
Let's take our cares and worries too
And cast them far from us.
Let's live our lives and breathe and sigh
And laugh aloud and plenty
We live one life and it should be
A joy for all who watch
Coz how can god if he exists
Want any less from us?

THE LANDCARE CONFERENCE
Lesley Podmore - Stanley Oct. 2011

I've been to the Landcare conference,
I'm really glad I went,
There were people from all walks of life,
With one purpose and intent.

We listened to all the speakers,
Their expertise and nous,
Some famous, others less well known,
But who we thought were grouse.

I've connected with some people
I haven't seen for years,
Who have spirit to keep on "keeping-on",
Despite those red-neck's jeers.

I've made some new connections,
Kindred spirits? ----- definitely,
And viewed inspiring projects
Concerning bush and farm and tree.

They even fed the lot of us,
With produce from our land,
And got several local fellows
To deafen us with their band.

So I've enjoyed the Landcare conference.
Yes I'm glad I've gone.
Enthusiasm's bubbling now
To forever forge right on.

JOB APPLICATION
Allan Jamieson

To: The Personnel Manager
        Ajax Mining Resources Limited

Re.: Your Job Advertisement

I was excited to find that you seek to employ a *Nuclear Nano-Layer Analyser Operator – Grade 3*.

I am sure that many applicants will attest to being experienced Nuclear Nano-Layer Analyser Operators at Grade 3 level. I am not such an applicant; as an older person, I am appalled at how brazen the younger generation has become. Everything with them is bluff.

While not having spent time operating a nuclear nano-layer analyser, I vouch that I could very quickly demonstrate proficiency, but so could any man-in-the-street, which brings me to the reason for my own job application: Yes, I do see a position for myself in Ajax Mining Resources (AMR). Let me explain:

• All modern analytical devices are simple to operate. A quick scan of the manual will reveal that the operator is expected to turn knob A with the left hand, while moving lever B with the right hand and observing the specimen to be analysed through the ocular enabler magnifier (also known as microscope) and, when the specimen aligns with the graticule (cross-hair), the operator presses a foot down on pedal C. The magic then happens automatically. How long would it take anyone to learn that? The answer is not very long.

• Thus, what AMR needs to employ is not another Nuclear Nano-Layer Analyser Operator – Grade 3, but someone with the entrepreneurial skills that I possess. Your job advertisement reveals that AMR now lacks these skills. Let me guess that AMR was originally either a Government-run laboratory, later privatised, or the founders of AMR came from some Government-run establishment. I mean, the use of Grade demarcations for jobs is only found in Government departments. As a consequence, AMR will lack entrepreneurial spirit.

• As AMR's Entrepreneurial Manager, I would make many changes. For instance, AMR would no longer employ operators, but would employ one clerk, whose job it would be to select casual workers on a daily, or even on an hour-by-hour basis, to perform the vast range of tasks for which I presume AMR is respected in the mining industry. Each worker would be hired for the work-at-hand and would be let go when that work was completed; e.g., at 4 pm or earlier.

• Pay would be on a piecework basis. Your current Finance Manager will assure you of the value of my proposal. When I was a manager, some decades ago, the cost of employing someone – over and above their direct salary or wage (the "on-cost") amount-ed to approximately 25% of said direct cost. Today, the figure is more like 60%. Thus, by making two employees redundant, AMR saves more than three salaries! Big bikkies! The piecework con-cept is loaded with other advantages. First, the worker has a clear incentive to process the work at hand fast – no time wasting. Cof-fee breaks will be history, and what's more, AMR will no longer have to accept that every hour each employee will stop work, go outside and smoke. Piecework is proven to be the most effective way of persuading people to stop smoking. [The lead provided by AMR's switch to piecework payment will be appreciated by the Minister for Health in the Government, who in turn will be welcomed as a hero in Cabinet for significantly reducing the size of the nation's Health budget].

• Do you catch my drift? It would surprise me if AMR needs to employ many people at all, hence the position of Personnel Man-ager will be redundant. Have you thought of this? With AMR's very generous redundancy scheme (four weeks' pay for every year of service), no doubt you will leave with a lump sum payout of the order of two years full salary and at a time when you are young enough to fully enjoy retirement: fishing on Tuesdays, golf on Wednesdays, minding grandkids on Thursdays, and a four-day weekend every week. What a life! If ever that life paled, I am sure that the clerk could be persuaded to take you on as a casual worker at a time of your convenience; the piecework pay achiev-able by a really proficient operator – if viewed on an hourly pay basis – is not to be sneezed at.

- Of course, there would be no need for a Finance Manager either. AMR's operations would be essentially on a cash basis. I am sure I can handle a daily trip to the bank to obtain notes and coins to pay the casual workers and to deposit the payments by the customers for our services, which will now be so much faster in being forwarded that customers will readily see the benefit themselves of paying in cash – no Accounts Section for instance.
- When I refer to a clerk, I do not mean to imply that the natural person to fill the position would be a clerk in the normal sense. This is because the clerk would be rewarded also on the piece-work basis – as soon as the daily operator hiring needs are filled, the clerk's task would end and payment would be made to him/her that day. Hence, it would be of benefit to AMR if the clerk was capable of making quick decisions. Might your boss be such a person? If not, I would approach an out-of-work Formula One driver. These fellows are only alive because they made quick decisions, and life must be awfully dull for them after their driving days are over. It ought not to be too difficult to pick up one of them for the clerk's role and their driving skills would ensure that my daily trip to the bank went like lightning.

Finally, I am known as a 'senior citizen', hence AMR would be able to take advantage of the Federal Government's incentive scheme – the one that pays employers to hire older people.

I urge you to seriously consider my application and, definitely, to hold off employing anyone to fill the advertised position of Nuclear Nano-Layer Analyser Operator – Grade 3; at least until your boss has made his (quick) decision.

I am
Yours truly,

Peter Principle

My motto: "What management pyramid?"

AUSSIE
Ant Dry

I recently read a story about an old woman who died in New York. She had been an immigrant to America from Eastern Europe after the Second World War, and she had lived in the same high rise apartment for decades.

As her children were sifting through her life collection of memorabilia and junk, they found the key to a bank safety deposit box.

The woman had been an industrious worker, eventually owning her own seamstress business. She had always lived frugally though, a fact that had embittered her children, who had always felt that they had lead a hard life. They suspected that she had squirreled hidden away a fortune, and the discovery of the safety deposit box key seemed to vindicate their suspicions.

With much excitement they went to the bank. As the estate beneficiaries they were granted access to the vault and were lead into a private room. The bank staff carried the safety deposit box in and left it on the table.

With fingers trembling with excitement, the eldest child opened the box. It contained a single sheet of paper, the elderly lady's most prized possession, the thing she valued above all else.

It was her certificate of citizenship of the USA.

As an immigrant to Australia from Zimbabwe, I understand how this woman felt.

My citizenship of Australia is my most prized possession. When my Aussie passport was ready for collection, I drove the 350 km down to Hobart to collect it, not trusting such a precious thing to the postal system. When eventually I held it for the first time, I was awestruck. I stroked the outside cover and opened it reverently. I felt the tears well up behind my eyes. I lifted it to my lips and kissed it, and gave whispered thanks to my new motherland.

Now, the average Aussie would role his eyes at this reaction to something so mundane, but this same average Aussie does not appreciate what is his by birth. He takes what he has for granted.

So what is it that makes me and the old woman from New York feel the way we do? What is it about either the US or Australia that makes them so wonderful?

Let's start with the small things.

It is wonderful that the power is always on. Okay, we have had some power cuts since we've been here, but when these have happened, there has always been good reason and Aurora has been very quick to sort out the problem – and we have known that and been comforted by it. In Zimbabwe the power was patchy at best. Its quality was so bad that the appliances would burn out when used.

It's wonderful that there is always fuel in the service stations.

It's wonderful that there is always bread on the shelves.

It's wonderful that water comes out of my taps any time I want it to.

It's wonderful that the Police are on our side and that they are there to help.

It's wonderful that you don't have to avert your eyes when you pass an armed soldier in the streets.

It's wonderful that the streets are clean.

It's wonderful that the garbage is collected.

It's wonderful that you can phone the tax office to make a run of the mill query and not thereafter be subjected to a full tax audit as you "must be hiding something"

It's wonderful that if your car breaks down, you can generally get it fixed without waiting for three months while you import your own spare parts as the dealer has none in stock

It's wonderful that there are road markings on the streets.

It is wonderful that the street lights work.

It's wonderful that the traffic lights work.

It's wonderful that I can be any religion I want and profess to any sexual orientation I might dream up and that officially I will be treated the same as anyone else.

It is wonderful that my property will not be taken away from me without compensation at the will of the government.

So much for the little stuff. What about the big things?

It was wonderful that my children's education was first rate. They went to a school in Australia, where the domestic science room had a full complement of stoves and that all of these worked. No one even considered them as a target for theft or vandalism. They had all the kitchen equipment they needed. Every child had their own set of school books. The sports room had a full set of all the equipment they might need. The music department had several sets of musical instruments. The kids were schooled in a system in which they knew that they would achieve a qualification that would be meaningful.

It was wonderful that the school Principal was not ever taken away by the Police for questioning as to why she was charging such high school fees.

It was wonderful that my children were able to attend a university that was not nearly always closed as a result of riots and consequent intimidation, and that their lecturers were always available for tutoring.

It's wonderful that my children are no longer growing up in an atmosphere where bribing officials is the norm, and corruption just another part of life.

It's wonderful that my children have a secure future and that I can be included in it. They can advance in their careers unhindered by any glass ceilings placed there by politics or race. They can have access to the "fair go" that WE Aussies love to espouse. They can plan for their future without fear of outside interference.

It's wonderful that I can live in a country that has hope and a future.

It's wonderful that if I have a beef with the government I can say so without fear of intimidation. I can write to the newspaper without fear of recrimination. I can actually go and see my local MP and he will not only see me, but will pretend to be interested. (I am a realist, I did say "pretend")

It's wonderful that despite the fact that we sound funny, and sometimes don't understand the slang, and have a few weird habits and mannerisms, we have been made to feel so welcome in our community. I suppose the members thereof acknowledge that they too were once immigrants.

I'm not sure what her previous life in Europe was like for the old lady who died in New York, but she knew that her changed circumstances were possible only because she had arrived in a great country.

She and I share that feeling.

Thank you Australia. Thank you for my life.

THE LONELY TREE
Dawn Meredith

My feet are wet. The ground is sodden. Water drips from the lichen covered rocks and trickles over my toes. My arms are weighed down with the damp, but I am unable to move, to seek shelter, for I *am* the shelter. Where I was planted will forever be my home.

I had friends, once, other oaks who sprang up after rains, reaching for the golden sun. We spoke of many things, between us, in our little grove. We laughed as fledglings tried their fluffy wings for the first time. We smiled as children played in our branches. We fell silent with sorrow when one of our own succumbed to the drought. Summers melted into fiery autumns. Silent, glistening winters warmed to the green of spring. Our trunks thickened powerfully with age, our hulking limbs stretched out their twiggy fingers to tempt the clouds with our shiny, capped fruit. We watched as many generations of humans passed through our grove. For centuries we watched the pantomime before us – their tiny, pathetic lives.

Now, I alone, survive. My trunk is gnarled and notched. My arms grow weak, my canopy is thinned. I am all that is left of the glorious grove that once bore witness to times both good and ill. I am old and I am lonely.

Our children should have long since grown to maturity, sheltered within our arms, sunning themselves and spreading blossom and seed for the next generation. But there are no young ones. They were harvested by the likes of that idiot farmer, McNicholl. His father and his father's father before him, all robbed the grove for their relentless fires and buildings, never thinking of the future. Who will protect them now? Who will provide shelter for birds to nest? Who will allow children to build swings and cubby houses? After I am gone, there will be no more oaks. No guardians of the land.

The rain trickles down my trunk, like tears. If only I could weep! I am the last mighty oak. Soon I shall fall into slumber and wake no more. My memories will die and rot beside me, for there is no-one to pass on my knowledge and memories to. No more oaks.

***

It is early spring and I grow tired. Soon I shall rest. My last acorns were harvested, my last leaves now struggle to open and shade the summer grass. By winter I shall be just a great, wooden carcass, for their wretched fires and houses. The sun tries to cheer me today, but I am so tired I no longer care.

Now comes McNicholl's son. Surely there cannot possibly be any more to salvage from the remains of the grove! The man is whistling merrily as his tractor pulls up. Oh, I can't be bothered watching any longer. Let it end.

What's this? He's speaking. Is he speaking to me? He is patting my trunk. I seem to remember he used to do that. To me it was yesterday, when he was a boy. Now he is digging near my old feet. What is he trying to do, dig me up? He whistles again. He's carrying something. It looks like… it is… it's a sapling, a fine young oak that he is planting, right by me! I greet it. Its voice is green and full of the juices of life. It is overjoyed to be here with me! Now McNicholl's son is planting another, and another! I am surrounded by slender young oaks, swaying in the warm breeze. Bees are coming to investigate. The saplings are all so excited. I feel my sap invigorated just by their presence. Oh, it feels so wonderful to have friends again!

Now McNicholl's son has put away his shovel and is patting me again. What is he saying? I lean down to hear his tiny voice.

"Old friend. This is my gift to you. You will not die lonely. I am owner of this land now and I reject my father's ways. There shall once more be a grove of mighty oaks."

FRITILLARY
Jennie Herrera

Sweet bright grasses fringed about a secret cove,
With little rasping voices, softer than the waves that curl,
Softer than the winds that trill a harmony across the dunes,
    Telling tales …
Butterflies brown and white, with lead-light marks upon their wings,
With tiny cooing voices, softer than terns, softer far than dolphin gulls,
Softer than a million sand midges with their tiny beating wings,
    Telling tales …
'We saw it there', 'it was so long ago', 'they passed the story on',
'Years and countless years', 'a hundred generations, *I* dare suggest'
'It flew, our ancestors claimed, like a thing possessed'
    Telling tales …
'How it cried' — 'like a beast bled, *I* heard', 'and all the while
A flapping', 'A noise, *my* family passed to me, like a clap of thunder'
— 'In a summer storm' — They drowsed together, in lush seed-head,
    Telling tales …

Victualling: Mr. Philobert Jenkins' account

That picher, sir? A fine ship, she were, on the
Nitrate run a while—carried forty men—and Shorty Sloane—
I've been with the firm near forty years, seen the fam'ly
Come an' go—but it's the ships you remember—Yes, sir?
Biscuits?—Mr. Mullins will serve you, sir—It were port
Not brandy for Lord 'amer's yacht—Beg yours—
Shorty Sloane? I remember 'im particular—Brought bad luck,
    The men said, casual-like—Couldn't see it meself—but never sailed,
    No sir—Salt, sir? Nine-an'-sixpence, that'll be—
They paid 'im orf, Shorty, left 'im in this port an' that—
Poor Shorty—couldn't leave the sea alone—
'e finally got a berth in 'obart Town—'e loved that ship,
An' Shorty weren't a sentimental man—a perfect clipper—
Pine—'aven't seen the 'uon pine, sir? Luv'ly yellow wood,

Made fine ships, that it did … Loved 'er like a son, they said,
Went overboard one night, left a note—
To give the ship good luck, 'e wrote, poor bloke—
Quaffed the cap'n's best French brandy, 'fore 'e done the deed,
No rum for Shorty Sloane when 'e set out for 'eaven, like—
An' you know what, sir? Didn't do no good … that fine clipper,
    Strong as they make 'em, plied the sea with perfect pitch, regal
like,
    Should've seen 'er, sir—an' ran before the wind, straight
    Into an open shore—some said it were the skipper at that
    Fine French brandy—but that weren't no comfort to poor Shorty—
    … Now your rope, sir, 'awser-laid … 'emp, sir, sisal or coir?

'The way it fell, like a stricken beast'; 'great gushing gouts, they
said',
'Not a story for the young' — 'And cries', 'More a bellow, in *my*
version',
'A wounded roar, *I* heard … like a dragon stabbed' — 'And then the
stalks broke'
    Telling tales …
'It had a name, they saw, in gilt upon its head'; — 'S.S. Fri---l--' —
'It wore away
With time, a shadow of a name'; the fritillaries gather round those
wormholes
In the weathered wood; a faint sweet fragrance still there about the
worn-out ribs,
    Telling tales …

DEAD TWIN: FOR GIANNA KRIEZOTOU
Graeme Hetherington

Eyes locking in recognition,
We became lovers overnight,
And after we had soothed the beast
Of longing for 'the other', she,

As we lay back to back, explained
The scarred lump on her tailbone: joined
To a sister, surgically freed
She alone survived. And when I

Reciprocated with my loss
Of a brother through jealous rage
I learnt it didn't correspond,
That her guilt was much more profound,

Beyond her mental powers to cope
Except through an obsession with
The horoscopes for gemini,
Whom she, a Greek, preferred to call

The dioskouroi, though in fact
They were capricorns. Her farewell,
In red lipstick upon the bed-
Room's dusty and cracked mirror was

Signed 'Castor and Pollux'. I found
Her with an old flame butting out
On her flesh, turning it to trays
Full of ash. Scornfully she said,

Of my shock, dismay and concern,
I didn't understand, to go
Away and write her epitaph,
And to console myself I did:

Gathering the scattered residue,
The fine grey dust of both, Zeus formed
Two stars from it, decreeing they
Should shine forever as The Twins.

WEDNESDAY'S CHILD
Dawn Meredith

Chaste of heart is Wednesday's child,
Pure and true and undefiled.
Untouched by powers of love and death,
Softer still than fairies' breath.

But who is this child, with no child is mind?
A mystery deep and undefined.
Old as Earth, yet young as dew,
ancient, yet forever new.

A spore, a bud, as yet unfurled.
A seed, untainted by the world.
A precious parcel, wrapped, alone,
Existing, yet unnamed, unknown.

Wednesday's child knows no ill,
Is not afraid, its debts are nil.
It has no gender, pulse or brain,
It has no voice, it feels no pain.

It trembles not in its cocoon,
Is not affected by the moon.
It feels no warmth, no cold, no sun.
Its suffering has not begun.

Its conscience lies untouched, unused,
Its trust has not yet been abused.
It feels no longing or regret,
Its troubles have not started yet.

For Wednesday's child is full of grace,
Though it has no human face,
It simply lies, in wait, unknowing,
Drawing lifeblood for its growing.

It does not cry, it does not fret,
Its destiny already set.
A course, a journey lies ahead.
It feels no fear, it knows no dread.

But slowly then, this child will wake.
And from its inward world will take,
The strength, the laughter, hopes and fears,
That will surface throughout the years.

Ahead the journey's end arrives,
As begins all human lives.
The seed has barely begun growing,
Wednesday's child begins that knowing.

Knowing truth and guilt and pain,
Peace and war, loss and gain.
All the gifts that life bestows,
The good and evil heaven shows.

Then love, as it begat this child,
Returns to earth, undefiled;
Remains the mystery's only clue,
Ancient, yet forever new.

RESISTANCE
Graeme Hetherington

I try to write at eighty-one
As Federer plays at thirty-six,
With evermore intensity,

An antidote to sensing that
The end is near, with a willed power
Stating deep hatred of the fact,

That would obliterate it, smash
Through to the peace another poem
Achieved or grand slam won might give,

If only temporarily,
Until it's time for proof again.
I know the darkness in his face,

The knitted furrowed brow and knot
Of concentrated fury when,
Like off tight racquet strings that could,

Worn thin from old age snap, my words
Slice bite spin skid, tear at the page,
Desperate to stay, as on a court,

Within the confines of the rules
With images pared down that still
Accessible excite and thrill,

As do balls bringing up the white.
While both of us just missing adds
To the toll of defeats and leads

To fear that all too soon we'll hear
The Invisible Umpire's call
Of 'out, game set and match to me!'

PIONEER ROAD
A Narrative in Ochre
Meg McLaren

CHAPTER ONE

An eclectic mix of humanity lived along Pioneer Road and in the surrounding bush land of this Northern region of Tasmania. They were much the same as you would find anywhere else in Australia or the world for that matter, surviving as best they could in these hard times. The wide, rutted street ran north to south through Settler's Rest, a township comprised of a scatter of houses, a general store, a school, a church and a cemetery with rusted iron gates intricately inscribed, 'Sleep Peacefully in the Arms of the Lord.' The Blue Partridge was at the southernmost end of the wide, dusty street, where a grassy embankment swept gently down to the river's edge and disappeared among tall rushes that lined the bank. It was a goldmine. Bill Jennings was a popular host and enjoyed a game of billiards and a beer with his regulars.

The orbit of Louisa's life was within the boundaries of the settlement. Sometimes she walked with Josh, following paths made by animals and loggers, winding between tall eucalypts their bark peeling in sheets, leaving behind smooth patches of pale amber and red. He had taught her so much; how to recognize the sound of a devil or wallaby rummaging in the undergrowth, a snake rustling the leaves, the gentle 'plop' of a platypus breaking the surface on a still pool of water. They were halcyon days. At night, after the sun dipped behind the forest, she read curled in an iron bed, flickering candlelight casting shadows around the walls and the plain wooden floor, a rag doll from childhood, with embroidered face, on the pillow.

Sometimes Stuart returned late, chockers after an evening spent at the Blue Partridge. Louisa would lie quietly listening to his stumbling footsteps, muffled by the forest of camellias near the front gate. When the floorboards shifted on the narrow staircase, she quickly blew out the candle lest he should see a faint glow around the door to her room. "She's got her nose buried in those Deadwood Dicks and Penny Dreadfuls again," he would shout at Edith. "You'd be better off teaching her to knit a pair of socks."

Edith, beneath the patchwork quilt, her back to the door, smiled. Sometimes it was hard to remember what had gone before. They had been in Settler's Rest for three years and their lives now had a predictable pattern, a soothing contentment. She let her thoughts drift back across the Strait, something she seldom did nowadays…..

It had been a cold mid-winter morning when Edith received word that Olga had died. The war had been over for seven months and the streets of Melbourne were filled with angry young men, trying to come to terms with what they had witnessed during the years abroad; unable to adapt to life as they once knew it.

Across the table Stuart ate quickly, busily gathering food with a knife and fork; an image of her lost happiness. What had attracted her to him in those days, when they were young? She would dash down Burke Street to meet him returning home, sprinkled with sawdust, her dark hair tied back with ribbon, eyes shining. "You have beautiful eyes," he would say kissing the lids of each one, holding her close.

Then in 1915, influenced by propaganda to do your duty and help Britain in her time of need, Stuart enlisted. Within a month he was on his way to Egypt. Louisa was just ten years old. He returned three years later, walked with a limp and was different in ways that Edith found hard to understand. She met him on the docks where he stood waiting, like a bewildered convict in a far-off land, in the same suit he had left in, now ill-fitting and hanging off his shoulders.

Olga's death changed everything. She willed her weatherboard cottage in central Tasmania to her niece, with one proviso; that Edith love and care for Jasper a large and rather dithering cat, who had been her constant companion.

"I'm not leaving" said Stuart. "Melbourne's a bonza place. What would I do with myself out in the middle of nowhere? What about Louisa?"

"It's Louisa I'm thinking of," Edith replied. "She's fifteen now. The change will do her good. A new beginning for us all."

Stuart was quiet. Edith was right. Louisa Grace, the product of their first year of marriage, when he loved his wife to distraction and could not keep away, was the light of his life. When the love cooled between Edith and him, mostly because of his drinking, Louisa saved him. Every day she waited for him to come home, and he would swing her up in his arms and play games with her. At night he sang songs of Scotland and told her stories of the Highlands and those bygone days when the Mackenzie's reigned supreme until, finally, her black lashes closed, like a blind when a cord is pulled. "If it weren't for you I might never come home," he'd whisper to his little silken girl and squeeze her so that, for an instant, the delicate cage of her chest was without breath.

Then, unexpectedly the house they had rented since before the war, was put up for sale. It seemed to Edith that fate had intervened. With no work and soon to be homeless, she insisted they should pack up and leave the city now they had a place of their own to go to.

In those bleak days prior to their departure, Louisa wandered aimlessly around the house between half packed suitcases and furniture. Everything was in confusion. The morning of their departure they were up before dawn. Neighbours arrived bringing parting gifts and food for the journey; biscuits, sandwiches, jars of jam with gingham print tops and lemon squash.

That evening the family stood on the upper deck of the ship that would carry them across the Strait and watched, bemused, as the city dissolved in the darkening shadows. The 'Nairana' steamed through the night, steadfastly battling winter gales and heavy seas. She was once a fighting ship and had played a part in the War. "Look at this!" Stuart called Edith and Louisa over to where a brass plate, affixed in the saloon, reminded passengers of her past glory. Stuart never spoke about the war but this shining plaque filled him with a sense of pride. He felt the faintest tingle of excitement, the first since they had decided to leave. "Maybe things will work out," he thought.

At dawn they sailed into the broad estuary of the Mersey, a hazy, pale slab of water, golden furrows rippling the surface and lapping against stone and rock. The ship moved slowly alongside Wood's Slip Wharf where sawmills roared and crunched around giant blackwoods and split palings were piled high against a long building. The waterfront was a hive of activity, men in grey and indigo, strung along the quayside, sweating, cursing and shouting as they heaved sacks of potatoes and crates of apples. The MacKenzies watched as an anchor was lowered into the murky water lapping at the pier.

"What's going to become of us here Edie?" Stuart, apprehensive and anxious once more, turned to his wife. "I'm a cabinet maker not a farmer."

"Don't you *what's going to become of us* to me, Stuart Mackenzie. If it weren't for your drinking and womanizing we wouldn't be here and you'd still be making cabinets." She paused, giving him a look that would turn the Devil to stone. "I'm warning you Stuart, you pull your weight or you can go back to Melbourne and your precious mates. Aunt Olga's given us a chance and I'm going to make the best of it. First time in ages I've seen Louisa so excited. This'll be the best thing for her."

"Hey, Murri, help the ladies." A voice, loud and forceful could be heard above the din.

Josh leapt over sacks of potatoes, to where the passengers waited, in a roped off area of the deck near the gangplank. He was tall, thin, his ribs exposed beneath a red and grey checked shirt. His face looked as if it had been darkened with charcoal. His lank hair was crudely cut. 'A pudding bowl.' A smile touched the corners of Louisa's mouth.

He held hard onto her hands as she stepped uncertainly across the thin strip of water between boat and pier.

"Part Abbo," someone murmured.

Louisa saw his eyes go blank, green flecks flashed on the surface like malachite crystals. The whispered insult made her heart bleed. She gripped his hands; breathless, transfixed by the power held in a single word. Then he was laughing and she with him, the moment gone. Nevertheless, the expression on Josh Murri's face at these words, was forever held in her head and she realized that she would never see things quite the same again and would look in another way at everyone who crossed her path. It caused her to look differently at Josh Murri now.

CHAPTER TWO

They stayed in The Palace Hotel on the corner of Rooke and Steele Street whilst putting their affairs in order. It was an imposing two-storey building. A wooden plaque at the front door declared it to be '*a home away from home.*' The moist, salt smell of the sea swept into their room on the second floor through a door opening onto a verandah. Stuart had befriended Josh Murri after the incident on the pier claiming him to be a hardworking and likeable fellow. A jack of all trades, he fixed houses, split palings, packed apples, dug potatoes.

A tentative friendship grew between the two men and Josh took to walking with the family at dusk, mingling with strolling sightseers on Victoria Parade or joining clusters of people listening to a brass band. Stuart persuaded him to follow them as soon as possible to Settler's Rest.

"There'll be plenty there to keep you occupied." He said throwing a friendly arm across Josh's shoulders.

One evening, after partaking of an excellent meal of spiced beef and hot plum pudding, Stuart made his way to the bar - a room like a dark inkwell, with paneled walls. A nude portrait simply ti-tled *Golora* had pride of place behind the counter. No one seemed to know what strange twists of fate had facilitated her journey from America to the saloon in the Palace Hotel.

Story had it that in 1915 the renowned American photographer Charles Gilhousen, pointed his camera at Golora and captured her forever, a small half smile on her lips. She had long, golden curls and tinted cheeks.

"Breasts that would feed a foal," John Dering was heard to comment whilst propping up the bar of an evening.

"A bleached hussy," Edith, with pursed lips, commented on the one and only time she ventured into this shadowy men's cave. "I feel as if I'm wading up to my ankles in muck!"

On this particular evening having knocked back a whiskey or two, Stuart struck up a conversation with John Dering who, he was told, lived in Settler's Rest. John had an open sided dray for hire, and agreed to transport the family and their belongings to their new home. During the course of conversation Stuart mentioned he would be looking for work.

"Plenty of that around," replied John. "I do a spot of logging with Forest Holdings, they're always looking for good men."

"Anything to do with wood and I'm yer man!" replied Stuart, beaming from ear to ear.

"Great! We'll soon have you sorted matey. What do you do for recreation?"

"Well I'll be buggered!" the tall bushman exclaimed to all and sundry when he heard Stuart also had musical abilities. "There's a few of us, six all told. Started a band a few years ago. We play Saturday nights in the Church Hall. Let's hear what you can do!"

Encouraged by the innkeeper, who'd been listening in on the

conversation, Stuart produced his cornet and began to play.

"You'd think it was Louis Armstrong," said a heavily bearded man, leaning on his elbows at the far end of the bar.

John was all smiles. "Wednesday's band practice!"

Edith couldn't believe their luck. "Didn't I say things would work out?"

She felt the clock had turned full circle and that all the events leading up to this moment were part of a bigger picture over which she had no control.

They said goodbye to Josh. "Don't leave it too long pal," were Stuart's parting words.

An arduous journey through wild bush country brought them to a low rise where the forest had been cleared and the family, looking back down the hill, could see the village. With a deft flick of his wrist John directed his team of horses onto a rough track that twisted around the rocks and trees. They bumped over potholes that would fill with water when the rains came - if they ever did - making the road impassable except on foot. There were several farms, timber homesteads set far back in clearings scraped between eucalypts. The right of way to each property was clearly marked. The horses, who seemed to know their way around, turned up one of these pathways.

It was that gentle time of year before the heat of summer sets in, rhododendrons bursting with spring colour, wild bluebells underfoot. A paling and shingle dwelling with a window looking out from the loft, revealed itself under a stand of tall trees. It stood on a small block extending down to the river, large enough to grow vegetables, and there were fruit trees. The surrounding yard was filled with all manner of agricultural implements, spades, forks, small ploughs, neglected and in need of repair. There was a cart and an old carriage in the stable. The house also needed patching up; rain rotted shingles hung low over the front verandah, where a large tabby lay sleeping. He appeared to be quite at home and barely raised his head, but purred loudly, when Louisa picked him up and snuggled her face into his soft fur.

Stuart looked around, pleased with what he saw. "I'll have to start right away on the window frames," He smiled stiffly as if he had forgotten how but, behind that smile, Edith caught a glimpse of the man he once was – warm, funny, passionate, loving.

She saw all this, but she also saw how it would be later; the house painted, a new barn and flowers springing up in the garden; crops growing where the land had been cleared. It was as if she moved in a dreamtime, floating wraithlike toward the dark shadows of the horizon. In her mind were images of men and women who had gone before, true colonials fearlessly embracing this ancient land; building a new world, a new history. She saw the whole picture and believed there would be a future for them here.

Later that first evening, the MacKenzies gazed out at the shadows shifting across a tangle of trees. The leafy smell was all around them. Stuart felt Edith's hip pressed warm against him, his arm circled her waist. She turned and he felt her fingers trace over his skin.

"We're home."

And he saw that she was smiling and crying all at once.

CHAPTER THREE

The Mackenzie's soon fell into the way of life in the valley. Their nearest neighbours, Ross and May Brooker, were friendly to the point of being intrusive. They appeared, as if from nowhere, whenever a job needed doing, be it scrubbing the floorboards or helping Stuart to repair the tools and equipment lying around the yard. May was a dumpy country woman, tree trunk ankles and a short neck. Ross was lean with a shock of grey hair and shifty eyes, electric blue. They sat at the front of the Church on Sunday nodding knowingly as Reverend Schlenk talked from the pulpit about neighbourly love according to God's Word. John Dering had warned Stuart about them the night they arrived.

"Sticky beaks Olga called them." John was serious. "She reckoned they were evil, especially May. Caught her out one night peeping in the windows; when she saw Olga she nicked off like a robber's dog."

"Can't be as bad as all that." Stuart replied.

"Well, don't say I didn't warn you!" John called out as the Clydesdales turned obediently and they headed back into town.

The following Sunday Edith had cause to remember his words. After the service was over and the parishioners gathered under an enormous Birch, sipping tea from dainty china cups, she overheard a cruel comment meant to harm.

"Things in that house no one should have in these hard times. A cabinet full of china, a musical clock, a bookcase filled with journals and the like." May sipped her tea, eyes moving slyly, skittering from side to side. "Where they got them I dread to think."

Edith looked around. In the midst of all this civility, no one seemed to be taking much notice of May's spiteful outburst; the women busily exchanging recipes and knitting patterns, the men standing apart talking of saw mills and steam engines and splitting logs. But, she understood then that May Brooker was a person who calls on another, her excuse being to share a cup of tea, but who really wants to see the way she lives and what her house is like.

"She's like a malignant troll in those Scottish stories of yours." She said to Stuart that evening. "I'll never talk to her as a friend again."

The sad thing was, she realized, that once you resolve to write somebody off, the friendship seldom resumes. There's no going back.

Josh arrived, a month or so after they had settled in. Stuart was delighted.

"There's a room at the back of the shed young fella. It's basic, but you'll find everything you need. Make yerself comfortable and come on over to the kitchen. Edith'll get you something to eat."

Within a short space of time, Stuart wondered how he had ever got by without him.

CHAPTER FOUR

And so the months passed quickly and life at the homestead became more structured and orderly. In the mornings Louisa and Josh went down to the creek to draw water. They chatted about this and that and soon became friends and were at ease with one another.

"Where are you from?" She asked one day, watching as he trawled a tin bucket through the ripples, careful not to slip on the reedy bank. There were times now when, in yearning lust, she lay in a clearing thinking of him and the unfamiliar swiftness with which he had reached out to kiss her that first time, his arm wrapping her in warm relief. Life would be unbearable without him.

She was staring at him, eyes wide beneath black lashes. Josh felt a tremor, he wanted her to understand. He felt as if he stood on a precipice high above the swirling ocean – a wrong move and he would fall. Nothing then but death!

"My mother Elsie, took up with a sealer on Flinders Island, an Irishman, Bill Murray. He loathed the slaughter of seals and so they moved to Blue Rocks on the west coast where he took up mutton birding and lobster fishing. I was born a year later and Elsie had her mind set that I should be at ease with both worlds." He paused. "Some days we wandered for miles along the shore, splashing through kelp forests, careful of tiny fish and seahorses playing there. She talked about the strange spirits that inhabited the legends of her tribe," Josh stopped remembering white, sandy beaches and towering ridges of granite; pink and grey, dappled with orange lichen. "Other times we walked along a track over Mount Strzelecki to the northern side of the island where her mob lived. There was an encampment, a sheltered spot, always a couple of skinny dogs wandering around, snapping at flies, hoping for a spare morsel. It was here I learned how to spear a fish, wading up to my waist in water, while Elsie sat with the women talking and weaving reeds."

Louisa nodded a picture forming in her mind of the women, their long, bony legs stretched out in front of them, breasts hanging down, swinging gently as they leant forward.

"When the sun dropped in the sky they seemed to disappear into their surrounds," Josh continued, "as if they were an extension of the shadows cast by fires that burned constantly. Then we made our way back home where Bill waited, composing his thoughts into poetic forms."

He looked at Louisa . "Did I tell you he wrote poetry?" She shook her head. "He taught me to read and write."

"So how did you come to Devonport?"

"Bill died attempting to reach a ship that had gone aground. Elsie died soon after, of a broken heart they say. I was brought to the main island and put to work on the docks." Louisa, pale and quiet in the twilight wanted to cry. She wanted to throw caution to the wind and grab hold of their dreams before they had a chance to disappear.

CHAPTER FIVE

Louisa's shift at the Blue Partridge was nearly over, she'd be home early to give Edith a hand with tea. She wanted to talk to her before

Stuart returned. After seeing Dr Schlenk that morning she was filled with helpless dread. All day she felt as if she were looking down on herself, suspended like an insect trapped in amber.

She called into Scotts General Store on the way home, Edith wanted some hose stockings. She picked up a pale yellow baby's coat with mother of pearl buttons. The finest cashmere, imported from the Scottish border town of Hawick where James Scott had completed his apprenticeship. Then, feeling herself observed, she looked up, straight into the curious and calculating eyes of May Brooker. Her stomach turned to water and she thought she would throw up right there in the shop. The cold, winter air worked its way into her heart and into her warm womb where the baby lay curled.

At home in the kitchen, Edith held her. "We'll get by. A new bub is nothing to be ashamed of."

"I haven't told Josh yet."

"Plenty of time for that. It's your father I'm worried about."

CHAPTER SIX

The sawmill shut down for the night. It had been a big day and the men were tired.

"You comin' down to the boozer Stuart?"

"Wouldn't say no to a glass of the old shearer's joy! Can't stay long though, the missus is cooking up a chook for tea. Hell of a job I had catching it too, damn thing jabbing at me with a beak like a razor blade, rolling its eyes, darting everywhere. You'd think it knew what I had in mind."

The Blue Partridge was warm, a wood heater going hell for leather in the corner. May Brooker, breathless, pulled at the bolt on the front door and a cold draught followed her into the pub.

"I've just bumped into Louisa Mackenzie and I'd bet my bottom dollar she's up the duff!!" She wallowed in the stunned silence that filled the bar. "Doesn't surprise me! The carry on between her and that Abbo! It had to happen."

"Seems like a hard working young fellow." Bill Jennings spoke up from behind the bar.

"Maybe so, but a white girl! Well spoken. He appears out of nowhere, the way they do, and look what's happened! Before we know it he'll have all his mates here."

No one saw Stuart standing in the doorway alongside Jamie Scott and John Dering. His face went white; then he turned sharply on his heel and strode back into the darkness without a word.

Josh had spent most of the day heaving logs. He loved the cathedral gloom of the forest at dusk, the smell of damp rot and oil released from trees, felled and stacked ready for loading. He was seated beneath an ancient tree, its trunk so large two people could not touch hands around it, whittling away at a piece of myrtle, his jumper dotted with wood shavings. Carving was what he loved best. Uncovering what was hidden inside a piece of wood just waiting to come out with his knife. This was a present for Louisa; a platypus, like the one they had seen last week heroically fighting the current as it made its way upstream. When they were apart he ached for her. Longed to circle her narrow waist and touch her hair. Just the thought of her was enough to transfix him with desire.

Stuart strode into the clearing. Through a red mist he saw the back of Josh's head, vulnerable where his hair grew down over a slender neck. He felt something underfoot, looked down and there it lay, heavy and solid. Stuart bent slowly and grasped the branch. He lifted his arm, a furious emptiness in his belly.

"Josh bloody Murri! I'm goin' to beat the living daylights out of you!"

Stuart was arrested and locked up for the night on a charge of disorderly conduct causing bodily harm. Josh was filled in on what had triggered the violent outburst. Louisa was distraught thinking of what could have been lost.

Edith was unforgiving. "Why don't you try fighting with your head sometimes instead of your fists? If Jamie and John hadn't followed you, I dread to think what might have happened."

Stuart was wretched under her gaze.

CHAPTER SEVEN

The community in and around Settler's Rest soon calmed down and slipped back into the usual run of things. However life within the weatherboard house on Robs Road had taken a turn. No longer the tight family unit they were before - the strain was palpable. Josh did not bring charges, but after talking to Louisa they came to a heartbreaking decision. The island now seemed to Louisa to be trapped in time, a rusty place, filled with narratives and secrets of the past. It would be too easy to become cut off and inward looking.

"No! No! Louisa, think of what you're doing! Melbourne's not the place to bring up a nipper."

Edith cried and pleaded in vain but there was no changing their minds.

Stuart said nothing – what could he say? Everything was different now.

So they were married in the old chapel beneath a stone angel, her hands clasped in prayer. May Brooker was not invited to attend.

The morning they were leaving Louisa went searching for Stuart and found him digging potatoes. When he looked up, Louisa noticed his face was streaked as if he had been crying and she thought it strange that he made no sound when he held her. She felt the baby move and she was engulfed by a wave of memories. An awareness of how much she loved him wrapped around her like a shawl and Stuart MacKenzie's daughter began to cry.

"We'll visit," her voice breaking; "This bub's gonna need a grandad."

CHIANG MAI - The Iron Bridge
Graeme Bourke

It's not that late as I stroll down Loi Khro Road in Chiang Mai, a northern Thailand city, as a matter of fact it's only ten o'clock. A nagging head cold has forced me to leave my partying friends to their eventual fate.

The temperature has dropped to a comfortable twenty seven as it tends to at night in the inland cities. With some lethargy and at the pace of a snail I walk along the narrow concrete street where the shop fronts border the edge of the road, some even encroach with an awning or addition or two. It's acceptable here so it seems, but I'm not sure about its actual legality.

I've seen marquees set up in front of houses taking up at least half the road when an official function is to be held at a residence, like a wedding or a birthday. It doesn't seem to faze the neighbours. Cars go around the block, motorbikes squeeze past the revellers with the riders smiling.

Walking on, I come to an Aussie pub on my right. You will find these throughout Thailand. They are a source of congregation for Aussie Expats and tourists alike. There's no air conditioning in the bar so the worn pale green wooden shutters of the windows are wide open as is the door. This allows the tepid air to flow freely. Patrons sit beneath swirling fans while they watch their sporting fixture, there is a section for rugby and another for AFL. I've always found rugby fans to be rather vocal and at times more noisy than their AFL recipients, no disrespect meant. Maybe they're just more passionate about the game.

You can purchase western meals here as long as the ingredients are available. The previous day my friends and I called in to watch some football (AFL) and partake of our first beer for the day. The menu looked rather inviting. I called the Thai waiter over and ordered the pork chops. One of my friends ordered the rissoles. In due course the owner, an Australian, approached us with his motorbike helmet in hand. He was full of apologies.

It seems the butcher who he obtained his pork chops from had failed to deliver and his staff earlier in the morning, when they had gone to the market, had forgotten to buy the mince. He was now on his way to acquire said supplies.

In no way did I feel any animosity toward the owner. I know Thailand, I know the people and their foibles. You can never take out the unpredictable Thai factor. You just accept it for what it is and keep a cool heart. 'Jai Yen' it is called in Thai. Needless to say we finished our beers and departed to a Thai restaurant further up the street that had delicious pork chops.

Twenty slow paces later I come to another bar on the left which was far more elaborate than the Aussie pub. It has glass windows and doors framed in aluminium. It also has air conditioning, which is a decided advantage when the daytime temperatures reach into the mid-thirties and beyond. They also have the sports channels. Reaching a four-way intersection I watch the flow of the traffic before making my way across and into a narrow lane that has barely enough room for a vehicle let alone a pedestrian.

A couple of days ago we were returning from a tour of the Ping River in a mini bus and on entering this narrow defile the driver of the van was forced to stop. There was an elderly lady with a pushbike struggling to get out of the way on the corner. I felt sorry for her. The driver calmly waited as the woman, with some difficulty, managed to move to the side so the bus could negotiate around the corner. All was well.

I make it safely through the narrow lane and reach the edge of the road that leads to the Iron Bridge, which spans the Ping River. To my left, on the esplanade are a couple of semi-roofed areas with a restaurant and band playing some rather tuneful music, I'm tempted to stop, but not tonight.

The Iron Bridge is a grey dreary looking structure. Even so it has some artistic merit. Five steel half arches cover the one lane bridge. To my surprise, as I make my way along the footpath and onto the bridge proper, I see groups of Thais on both footpaths.

As I approached the dozen or so young Thais, I realised they weren't interested in my passing. Two girls are sitting in the middle of the footpath. One is texting on her phone. The other is sipping some soup through a straw from a plastic bag. It's a common way of selling takeaway soup here. They are oblivious to the fact that they are blocking the footpath. Checking for vehicles I step onto the road and go around them.

It seemed rather strange to me why they were gathered here

on the bridge. Did it hold some religious or historical significance? It's possible as Chiang Mai is some seven hundred years old; at least, the brick wall and moat that surround the old city is. The moat and sections of the wall can still be seen today. Parts of it have been reconstructed, some of it has disappeared completely and other sections are just mounds topped with vegetation or grass.

The bricks are a rich earth colour ranging through orange, red, brown and paler versions of each. They are longer than a standard brick and rather flat. It must have taken millions of these to build the original wall. It's a wonderful mosaic of the past.

Moving on I see a young man leaning on the rails of the bridge typing away on his phone which hovers precariously in the void over the muddy Ping River. One slip, one mistake and it would be gone.

I reach the end of the bridge and cross the road to the small laneway leading to my hotel. On the right is a construction site, a skeletal concrete structure that looks rather forbidding in the darkness. The security guard at the hotel is distracted with his phone as I arrive at his tiny unpainted rough wooden hut where he is ensconced. He looks up, passes me the key and bids me goodnight.

At breakfast the next morning as I'm dished up a pair of hard-boiled eggs that take some cracking, I meet my companions and am instantly entertained by their versions of the previous night's antics. I enquire of them if they noticed the people on the bridge as they come back to the hotel. 'What bridge?' replied one of my friends with a laugh, it was a stupid question. I should have known that they would have been in the glazed world of intoxication.

Later that morning I went back to the iron bridge and took some photos. In the daylight it was just another picturesque bridge. The footpaths looked desolate and empty, but that evening as I strode back over the iron bridge the young Thais were there again, grouped on both sides. I stopped and peered into the slow-moving muddy water of the Ping River that flowed to Bangkok and beyond.

There was a presence here, I could feel it. Did this particular location have some ancient significance? Whatever, it was obvious that something drew the young Thais here. If you are ever in Chiang Mai go and visit the Iron Bridge and I sure you will sense the peace, the solitude and reverence of the site just as I did.

THE LAST DAYS OF ROGER EAST
Jennie Herrera

"I think you should leave Dili now, Roger. It would be better—safer—for you."

The older man shook his head. "No. But thanks anyway. I'll stay a bit longer."

Someone across the room protested. "You're crazy, man! You know what they'll do to you?"

"No. What?" he asked blandly, the ghost of a smile round his mouth. It wasn't that he had any illusions left.

"You know what they did to your *compatriotas* in Balibó when they came across the border. They say—Australians! You communist pigs! You help Fretilin! Then—Pow! Pow!—all dead. Guido told me." The speaker grimaced and spread his hands as though to draw in more listeners. "You know they say on Kupang Radio you are communist too?"

Roger East nodded. "Propaganda is a strange thing, the way it can make sane people believe absurd things."

"I don't believe a thing they say! Never!" someone else broke in.

"Just as well," East agreed, mopping his neck. The humidity in the room was intense and it was compounded with something he found harder to define—a strange mixture of fear and courage, apprehension and frayed nerves.

"What was it you told me you did in Australia one time?" Xavier joined in the brief exchange which followed several hours of hammering out strategy—hours in which Roger East had listened carefully and keenly, for the mixture of Portuguese and Tetúm and occasional English had both cloaked and clarified the needs and priorities of this, the world's newest nation, as, day by day, the claws and fiery breath of Operation Komodo shut it off from the outside world.

"I used to be Press Secretary for a well-known Country Party politician—the usual training ground for radicals and communists, you know." But the irony in his joke was missed and already a different subject was being discussed earnestly.

"Are Ford and Kissinger still in Jakarta?" someone had

asked.

"Today and tomorrow I think—"

"And then it will be—goodbye, Mr President, so nice of you to call—and then they will be here in their thousands—and Boom! Boom! Dili goes up in smoke—"

"—and Mistair Ford, he say, what nice mens there, so kind, so polite, and he go home to Washington all happy."

Roger East permitted himself a brief smile—glad they could still find the ability to laugh with tragedy staring them in the face—and stood up, stretching his stiff limbs and putting away his notebook and pen. Then he eased himself out of the crowded room.

Mário tapped his arm lightly. "Roger, come with us when we go. You know we can't hold Dili."

Again he turned down the earnest request. But it touched him deeply—their concern for his safety. He went down the stairs and out into the still air of early evening.

It was true what they were saying upstairs. With the American President gone from Jakarta and the rainy season well on its way, how many days' grace could they have? Two? Three? A week?

It was the evening of the fifth of December.

*

He cut across the park, sunk in pessimistic reflection. The encircling mountains had deepened into beguiling purple shadows. 'Come to us,' they seemed to whisper, 'come to the mountains. We'll hold you in our bosom, deep in our fastness. Come.' He shook off the seductive thought and walked on. There were still people out on the streets and in the bar next to the TAT office. But it would be dark soon and the lights would be hidden.

He turned along the seafront road, the flapping of his thongs loud over the gentle hiss of waves on sand. Old rusting Japanese hulks from the war, a different war, spread their shadows across the beach.

They're no more than kids, most of them, he thought bitterly. Poor beggars. They've been asked to run this country, pull it up by the bootstraps—and they haven't been given a bloody chance.

He walked on slowly past the silent buildings, the Câmara Municipal, the Taiwanese Consulate, the gleaming white statue of the Virgin on her pedestal. Dear Lady, do your stuff, he mused. Heal the sick, tend the wounded, do your miracles, then I'll believe again.

God knows, they need some miracles.

The bar at the Turismo was open and the Bee Gees blared from the juke box but he went straight upstairs. His room was closed and stuffy and he crossed to open the window and let the first faint stirrings of the sea breeze in. But he felt curiously reluctant to sit down at the typewriter and begin putting his notes in order.

A strange almost Kafkaesque mood seemed to settle and grow on him as the hazy red sun disappeared below the horizon and redrew the cathedral tower as a silhouette against the feathery blackness of the palms.

Lights winked faintly far out, where the rose and silver sea arced between the lighthouse and the steepled point of Ponta Fatocama—a jailer who guarded, not with jangling keys heavy on a rusty ring but with pinpricks of light as alluring and as deadly as a will-o'-the-wisp in the tropical dusk.

He turned away with an involuntary grimace and lowered the heavy blind before switching on the light and settling himself at his table to begin work on his next dispatch. Tonight, the jail. This morning they had been rabid communists ready to swarm all over their neighbours. Yesterday they had been claimed as brothers, as fellow victims of European colonisation. Tomorrow ...

Next morning he breakfasted early and went out. Already the day had begun to feel clammy, with shreds of clouds gathering over the bare outlines of hills green-tinged from the first storms. Soon the rains would be here in earnest. As usual he had his camera and notebook with him but today he could summon little enthusiasm to question or photograph people fleeing to the safety of the mountains, perhaps because of a premonition he would never see them again.

But he kept that thought to himself later when the President, Xavier do Amaral, came up to speak to him. His dark eyes behind thick glasses surveyed East's face, florid in the unforgiving heat, sympathetically. And his request was equally sympathetic: at least move from the Turismo to the rear of the city. He offered what sanctuary his own house could provide.

But he expressed no surprise when East politely declined his offer, only regret. And rather than waste time in persuasion he went on to talk over information coming in. Indonesian troops were already at Atabae, well inside the border, and had set up a command post there.

Amaral handed a leaflet to the journalist. It was propaganda, no mention of brotherhood this time, its message undiluted by ethical adornment or regard for the truth. Fretilin, the Indonesian blurb stated confidently, would fall within five days.

East put it in his pocket. "Thanks." The underlying message was clear: the Indonesians were on their way.

He spent the remainder of the morning talking to those who had chosen to stay—the Chinese shopkeepers, administration officials, Falintil troops, villagers on the outskirts. Then he returned to the hotel to take several tablets and lie down briefly. Perhaps it had been madness not to join the stream of people winding their way up into the scrub-covered hills. But would they be safer? The government planned to fall back to Aileu to regroup. But was it only prolonging the agony? Aileu with its little grey monument to its war dead—'*Por Portugal contra o Invasor*'. But Portugal was nearly gone and it was a new invader and once again Timor would mourn. Yet it wasn't that simple, was it? A brief dispatch, confined, crackling, could not begin to tell this complexity.

They said Aileu had been attacked by men from West Timor, churned to fever pitch with *sake* and wild promises, given old Dutch rifles by the Japanese, sent yelling at the small garrison, stabbing and killing its commander Captain Freire da Costa and his wife. Timor was twice hurt by the priorities of distant generals who found they could make the tribesmen of the hills do their fighting for them. No brotherhood. Because far away men—in Lisbon, in Amsterdam, in Tokyo, in Canberra, now in Jakarta—had decreed that brother should fight brother.

And the Portuguese governor, Lemos Pires, sat wearily in Ataúro because Jakarta had spread the rumour Indonesians disguised as Fretilin would kidnap him as an excuse for their invasion when their secret manoeuvering of the UDT coup in August failed to create sufficient chaos to hide their blatant entry, a law-and-order entry, as illegitimate as Hitler's stooges dressed up in Polish clothes at a different border. But now with the five journalists killed in Balibó and carted the thousand kilometres to Jakarta, instead of simply into the care of the Red Cross here in Dili, without a word of condemnation from Canberra or London—Jakarta knew excuses were not needed. No one would interfere. Not brothers certainly, those men in Australia who had decreed the dropping of FELO leaflets on Timor thirty years ago to say 'Your friends do not forget you'; but friends, fine fair-weather friends, where were they now. But then they'd been equally willing to drop leaflets 'Remember! Keep away from the Japanese or we will be forced to attack you!'; all the while knowing it was coerced and starving Timorese who laboured to build the Japanese airfields and roads. There had never been choices then. Now there were. Would Canberra respect the choice they'd made only nine days ago? Independence.

His fingers sweated in the damp heat, every so often he stopped to wipe his neck, (like Darwin; not like Eumungerie in rural New South Wales... the burning heat in that little Depression shack by the railway, heat and dust, tin and hessian ... poverty) as he worked on his next Reuters dispatch—'The residents of Dili have been making a quiet exodus to the hills as the security situation deteriorates. Tonight Dili is silent and almost deserted. For the fourth night a blackout is in force and the beaches and sidestreets are guarded by heavily-armed troops ... '

Conscientiously, he went through the various scraps of new information (should he go to the border, to Atsabe, Balibó, Maliana, try to go), the snippets of "human interest", details of who remained and why, all that the day had yielded for both his own news agency and the wire service—but he couldn't help feeling whatever usefulness they might once have had was gone now. Because now there was only the waiting.

He went out again in the early evening to take his messages to the Marconi centre, walking slowly through streets which had once buzzed with thousands of young travellers from the West, villagers from the mountains with laden ponies, Portuguese officials and conscripts. Go, you idiots, he thought, why guard an emptying city? Let it crumble away, let the stray dogs welcome the Indons, lick their boots, pee on their knife-edged creases—their tanks—their Janus faces. Hell, who cares about a few buildings?

But its indolent Mediterranean charm surrounded him with a gentle persuasive longing and he began to whistle, a younger man, brashly self-confident, whistling through the silent truce of a Cypriot night ... he shrugged away the memory for what did it have to do with this middle-aged man plagued with dull cramping stomach pains—and the knowledge, clear tonight, that he would never see Cyprus again? Never see anywhere again. These, my children ... But that was the trouble. They couldn't give up the city without a fight because it was too *new*. Almost every building had risen out of the rubble of another war. The cathedral had once stood here, in the centre of Dili, but the RAAF had bombed it and the Japanese had destroyed the remains of its twin towers, saying the Australians used it to guide their bombing runs over the dying town; the new cathedral away to one side now, new roads and parks and monuments.

He hurried on from the radio office so he could see off the members of the Red Cross team at Dili airfield for their short flight across to their base on Ataúro island. By the time he'd retraced his steps to the Turismo the island was disappearing into the velvety grey of the night. The clouds had cleared again without loosing a drop of rain and the evening star was out. And was that a light, a star, a phosphorescence, on the horizon? Are my eyes playing tricks? Or are they coming? After a minute of intense concentration he turned into the hotel courtyard, still unsure.

The place was quiet. He was the only guest left. So why stay, he asked himself. What good could it do? But a sense of duty intervened. He was there for one purpose and one purpose only: to get the truth out. Beyond that did anything matter? You shall know the truth and the truth shall make you free.

He ate a small meal without appetite then went upstairs, feeling listless and tired. But it was a drawn frayed tiredness and he was inclined to think there'd be no sleep for him tonight, not with the growing certainty the dragon was creeping slowly inshore. You shall know the truth ... and the dead shall bury their dead ...

He had no wife, no children waiting anxiously for his return. Only brothers, Bill and Doone, and his little sister and they had their own lives to lead. But perhaps he'd made a terrible mistake. There was no way he could dispatch the truth—if he was dead. He began to tidy his belongings and pack them, till only his typewriter and camera remained—and troubling thoughts about truth and freedom and his duty toward people who still placed their faith in him, that he alone could tell the world.

Tomorrow was Pearl Harbor day, he thought vaguely. Which anniversary? He did some sums while he took off his shoes and lay down. I was nineteen when I joined the R.A.N. I served my country as best ... what will they do for me when I am killed ... here ... 'Your friends ... ' Perhaps he could work it into a story ... after all, Suharto had collaborated with the Japanese until it became clear Japan was not going to win the war ... perhaps the parallels were important ... the wharfies, our brothers in Indonesia ... perhaps nothing from the past mattered ... because brothers, friends, fellow citizens, were meaningless words in the end ... he slept ...

The sound of aircraft in the night snapped him awake again. Then muffled explosions jerked him up, to reach clumsily for his shoes in the semi-dark; the earth shook, the sounds closed in, and he cursed himself for sleeping. His body protested as he snatched up his bag and stumbled downstairs.

Already the colour of dawn was on the horizon and he was out in the courtyard. Where once he'd sat relaxed, talking, sipping a glass of firewater, now the air was filling with dust and smoke. His next dispatch began to form—'The town is being shelled from off-shore positions. Aircraft flying overhead—dropping paratroopers'— or were they vultures plummeting to a body which would refuse to die—

And I'm a bloody sitting duck here, he thought, as he turned to run with a screaming in his ears. The blacked-out city was growing bright—a livid unhealthy glow, as the thatch roofs of Timorese houses caught fire. Dry scrub behind the shoreline flared into short-lived bonfires.

One grim resolve filled his mind as he ran, sweating from exertion and fear—finish the bloody dispatch and send it before you're cut off—a short message, that's all you need—the invasion is under way, the date, the time—his mouth felt dry.

Hell to the noise! They're not going to hear me! He struggled to stay calm as he read out his last message for Darwin. Around him the dawn was dissolving into a maelstrom of noise—terrifying ear-splitting noise—a banshee who'd come screaming in with the sunrise—

But his message was out and, for now, he could do no more. There was no reason to return to the Turismo and he turned instead towards the rear of the city, his shoulders slumped, still carrying the case of the dispossessed ...

Postscript: The way in which Roger East died was first brought out by two Chinese refugees who testified in the late 1970s that he was shot on Dili wharf on the 8th December, 1975, by members of the Indonesian Army's 501 Battalion. His death has never been fully investigated, nor has anyone ever been charged.

Yet, somewhere round the island for which he gave his life lies an unmarked grave inscribed in unseen letters. You shall know the truth ...

NEW ZEALAND MEMOIRE
Graeme Bourke

Many years have passed since I climbed the mountains of New Zealand hunting for deer. I have fond memories of my hunting expeditions and those memories were rekindled when I began looking at some old photos of a trip to New Zealand back in March 1978.

There were six of us, all keen deer hunters with experience at hunting Fallow deer in Tasmania. Two of the group, Eric and Warren had hunted in New Zealand before. It was from their know-how that we began organising a trip to the South Island to hunt for Red Deer; it would take twelve months of meticulous planning. We tried to allow for every scenario that could possibly happen, all except one which would ultimately make the trip a little more challenging. The other members of the party were Tim, Peter and Graham.

It was midnight before we cleared customs in Christchurch. As we were flying out to Queenstown early next morning, we decided to stay at the airport for the night rather than try and find a hotel at that late hour. Sleep was very hard to come by as the excitement of being in New Zealand, the uncomfortable seats and the whining of the vacuum cleaners at three in the morning kept us awake.

It was around this time that someone discovered a local newspaper that hadn't been claimed by the cleaners. The headlines were numbing as we read that in the last twenty four hours New Zealand had been hit by a severe low pressure system. Subsequently, it had dumped 24 inches of rain (approximately 600 mm) over the area on the west coast where we planned to hunt. All the local rivers were in flood. A sense of despair fell over the group.

We flew out that morning to Queenstown via Mt Cook, but because of the high winds and low visibility we couldn't land. The plane circled for a while much to the detriment of the passengers who began vomiting on masse. Somehow my stomach held its own. On arriving at Queenstown, we booked into our guest house on the side of the hill overlooking the lake and then we spent the rest of the day organising food and equipment. The next morning, on a crisp clear day we boarded our light plane for our flight to the Waiatoto River.

I was immediately in awe of the magnificent scenery. Glaciers like rivers flowing, etched with crevasses, wound their way around inconceivably old peaks. We were so close that the wing tips of the plane seemed to almost reach out and touch the mountain ranges. Peering down, I could see the wide yellow grassy plains between the steep mountains that had been carved out by the swift flowing rivers. Flowing patterns of grey stone on the riverbeds were interwoven in seemingly artful outlines. The thickly wooded hillsides rose abruptly to meet with the pale snowgrass, the grey rocky cliffs projected into the air like hillside forts and the craggy snow covered peaks reached even higher into a transparent sky..

The plane twisted and turned as it threaded its way between the peaks until we came to the Waiatoto River. Cautiously, the pilot circled the landing strip, which we could plainly see on the valley floor below. The signs weren't good. The grass strip had been under water. The pilot steered the plane away from the valley, he wouldn't risk a landing on the sodden earth. Now what, we wondered? Twelve months of planning had just been thrown out the window.

Eventually, we ended up in a place called Kea Flat, which was situated in a wide valley with sloping hills. This would be our home and our hunting ground for the next week or more. It looked like good deer country.

The hut at Kea Flat was a very basic affair with rough wooden bunks, an open fire and galvanised iron for cladding. Our only luxury was an outside clothes line. To make matters worse, there was only room for four people to sleep in the hut. Graham and I were happy to sleep in his two man tent outside.

For the next few days we traipsed the hills, climbed the cliffs, followed the trails and searched the woodland, but not one deer did we see. Personally, I felt that there were deer here, call it a sixth sense, something that most hunters possess. But where were they? Frustration was beginning to set in. A whole year of planning had gone into this trip. Were we doomed to failure? It wasn't looking good.

Climbing high one particular day, I took time out to just enjoy the scenery. There were no signs of civilisation here, no roads, and no rectangles of man's making. The serenity and peacefulness of this place was something to behold. The mountain peaks were silhouetted against the grey-blue sky and far below me lay the horizontal valley floor. To me there is something primeval about sitting on the side of a mountain with the immediate world below and in front of you.

I could be a king surveying my kingdom, I could be an adventurer having just climbed a mountain and found a hidden valley, but alas, I was but a simple hunter enjoying what kings and adventurers long before me had experienced.

On the fourth day we decided to spread out along the valley and then climb up through the forest to the snow grass. We hoped that by covering more territory we might run across some sign, and there was always the chance that one of us could put a deer to flight across someone else's path.

With the .270 rifle held firmly under my arm I pushed my way through the forest, having lost sight of my companions on either side. I moved very slowly, stopping every now and then to listen to the silence of the forest. Darting eyes scanned everything about me, I felt the tension, and the hairs on the back of my neck were rising. It was the old familiar feeling. I knew the hunt was close.

Through the trees above me and slightly to my left was a large patch of rocks and boulders, it looked like debris from a washout where heavy rain had scoured the hillside. This was a likely place for a deer to cross. Instinct told me to stay out of sight as I moved up the hill slowly in a semi crouched position, each step carefully planned. Every subtle movement was slow and deliberate. I stayed on the edge of the forest with the open area of rubble clearly visible in front of me.

Then I saw her. The red flanks reflected in the sunlight as she made her way across the open stretch of ground. I eased the rifle to my shoulder and brought the scope to bear. The deer dropped into a hollow and out of sight. My heart was pumping as I sprinted out into the open to a point where I could see the other side of the depression. Precious seconds ticked by, I was shaking and the rifle seemed to be wandering all over the place as I put the scope on the spot where I expected the deer to rise out of the hollow. And sure enough, she did. The shot echoed through the hills as the recoil lifted the rifle. I could see that my aim was true. The 130gn bullet had entered the chest of the deer and it was a clean kill.

It was a happy bunch of hunters in the camp that night as we wasted no time skinning the hind and making a big pot of stew, as we had eaten no meat for a week. The conversation was jovial. It was as if everyone had been rejuvenated from the misfortunes that had preceded us. Unfortunately, this euphoria only lasted for a couple of days. Everyone slowly became depressed at the lack of action, to the point where we were just hanging around the camp in a dejected state of mind.

One day Graham and I were sitting outside enjoying some sunshine. Grey smoke was billowing out the chimney of the hut; we decided to liven things up a bit. The other four were in the hut sleeping and reading. We made sure the door to the hut was closed and then we climbed up to the top of the chimney and covered it with a piece of tin. Then we sat back and waited.

We heard the rumbling in the hut, just like the noise a rabbit makes as it flees its burrow. Our mates jostled each other for room at the door. Graham and I laughed at the comic actions of our friends, as they coughed and spluttered, cursed and laughed with us.

The next day saw a sombre bunch of blokes packing their gear away, for tomorrow the plane would arrive to take us away from this little piece of heaven. We had timed our food supplies well, there was virtually nothing left.

That night as we settled down for our final sleep in the wilderness, we detected a rise in the strength of the wind gusts. The next morning the wind was still blowing strongly when the plane arrived. He flew over us, waved his wings and then soared off into the sky. It was too dangerous for him to land in the windy conditions. What more could go wrong on this trip? Everybody moped about, grumbled and began unpacking some of the gear that we would need for another night's stay.

Far from being despondent, I picked up the rifle, loaded some ammunition in the magazine and promptly informed my friends that I was going hunting. We had been granted one more day, I was going to try and take advantage of it.

The forest here ventured close to the river bed that was probably some three hundred metres wide. It was interspersed with tiny rivulets branching off like arteries from the main stream. Rounded white boulders worn smooth by countless years of washing reflected the morning light. I stepped back into the edge of the rain forest and moved on slowly, keeping my eyes moving backwards and forwards, sometimes peering into the dense forest, and sometimes looking across the river.

Every now and then I would stop, listen and study the ground in front of me. Then I saw the unmistakable fresh footprints of a big deer in the grey coarse sand on the edge of the river. The hairs on the back of my neck were standing up. The deer had come out of the forest, strode out onto the wet sand and then returned. Slinking back into the cover of the forest, I proceeded to walk at a snail's pace, tension filled the air. I hadn't gone twenty metres when something made me turn and look back.

He was standing on the edge of the river bed looking majestic with a forlorn stare in his eyes as he peered across the wide expanse of riverbed. I sensed that he wanted to be on the other side. The red ruffled flanks shimmered, his mane prominent on his neck, the wide thick antlers reached into the air like the prince he was.

This was the moment of truth, the culmination of a year's planning and three weeks of frustration all brought down to one finite moment. I took a couple of steps forward and knelt down. I was becoming rattled with buck fever. Taking a deep breath, I let the cross hairs fall on his powerful shoulders, I was only about thirty metres away and the deer hadn't seen me. I lifted the crosshairs slightly deciding to go for a neck shot. Squeezing the trigger, the rifle bucked and the red stag fell where he stood. Standing up I walked forward and stared down at my prize, a worthy eight point red stag. I returned to the hut with a smile from ear to ear as I recounted the event to my friends.

Despite the lack of success, the camaraderie between us all was probably the best part of the trip, along with the scenery. All of us would have fond memories that we could hold onto and recall in our old age. In a way, I was lucky, I shot two deer.

WHAT'S IN A NAME? (2)
Graeme Hetherington

(For the Skeggs-Hetherington Clan)
Entitled only by the dash
That joins in legal documents,
And through a step-great grandad to
Be called Hetherington, Skeggs alone,

Its sound uncushioned, unabsorbed,
Thick, harshly blunt, terminal when
Unadorned by its better half,
Is, like it or not, my blood-name.

And there's the rub, since it's not just
That this appellation, suppressed
Till values changed, has brought to light
My convict past, direct kinship

With others so abruptly dubbed
As Fox Sparks Lynch Crack Maggs; nor that
It rhymes with dregs and brings to mind
The murderous Bill Syke's cringing pie-

Bald stunted cur, or even worse,
The onomatopoeic jerk,
The dislocating jolt and snap
Its brutish shortness sets off in

My ear as when lifts hurtling down
Come to a sudden shocking stop,
As though I was born to be hanged.
More painful is that I have no

Inherited genetic claim
To the aesthetic of a three
Or four-syllable elegance,
Depending where the stress is placed.

VALLEYFIELD MURDER
Allan Jamieson

When I entered the pub, I spotted two of my friends at a table to my left. They seemed to be in an earnest conversation.

"G'day. It has to be my shout by the look of your glasses."

I went to the bar, bought three beers, and then returned.

"Now, what's got you blokes so excited?"

"Brian reckoned he's solved that Valleyfield murder, but he's way off – I solved it five years ago."

Brian wasn't taking anything lying down. "No", he shouted pointing a finger at Mick. "You overlooked the two key pieces of the puzzle – that's the only way *you* can dispute my explanation! Take *them* into account, which I've done, and there's *no* other possible solution."

I sat down and sipped my beer, before offering the pair my initial thought.

"It's a bit hilarious, I reckon, that you're berating each other over who's *solved* that mystery, or who's explained *what* took place, when the police still haven't come up – eight years later – with a motive or a culprit. Don't you think you're each deluding yourself, and being rather precious into the bargain?"

"Says who?" glared Brian. Mick smiled. "He's real sensitive today, isn't he? I suspect there's an ulterior motive lurking somewhere; maybe he's spreading false theories around, because he's worried that the cops are onto his tail."

If I hadn't slammed my arm down on the table top, Brian would have upended it, with the beers, in Mick's lap.

"Steady on you two. Mick – you're accusation needs backing up – or withdrawing. And just how many beers have you two had?"

Silence reigned – briefly. Before they could get at each other's throats again, I asked, "How did this conversation start? Who was first to mention Valleyfield?"

"I drove through Epping Forest ten days ago", Brian said, "and I saw the road sign pointing to Valleyfield airfield. It reminded me of the murder, so I dug out the newspapers of the time and today I told Mick that I had it solved."

"Yeah, and I'd done the same thing five years ago and I

couldn't resist telling Brian he'd 'missed the boat'."

"Ok", I said, "let's get the basics agreed. What I recall is that the girl – in her 20's, wasn't she – was found dead in a roadside ditch by a local farmer. The autopsy didn't find any injuries to her body, other than at the head. She hadn't been violated. Have I got that right?"

They nodded.

I added, "I'm not sure any more was ever published, was it?"

Brian said, "I found a lot more – and that's why I disagree with Mick. He overlooked some facts."

"Alright, Brian; you tell us what you learned from your research and, Mick, you keep quiet."

"The police described three suspects, though not all at once. The first bloke was an itinerant farm worker who the police said had come to Tasmania for the fruit picking season then stayed on. He was seen thumbing a lift on Valleyfield Road. I reckon he was an easy pick – you know, foreigners and especially drifters are easy to suspect. Anyway, it wasn't long before the police stopped searching for him and a while later they began to describe another bloke and, soon afterwards, another man. The *impression* was given that both these men could have been with her when she was murdered.

"That's where the police investigation stalled; other clues did not come to light; at least, not at the time."

"Who was she?"

"From Hobart – not wealthy and estranged from her parents. She frequented bars and pubs and a few nightclub operators recognised her. Nobody ever explained how she came to be in Valleyfield – no evidence of being murdered elsewhere and brought to that ditch, and no sign of a fight at the ditch either."

"Could she have hitched a lift from the wrong bloke?"

"A strong possibility, but the police didn't have any success at the time when they pursued that line."

"Ok – did you know all this, Mick?"

"Yes, and I say I solved the mystery five years ago."

"Alright! Tell us – and Brian, you keep your cool while he does."

Mick smiled. "There's no debate that the only real explanation had to involve her getting into the wrong car. I reckon she'd decided to try her luck in Launceston and so she put out queries at her Hobart haunts. Eventually a bloke said he was driving there and he offered her a lift. She probably thought she was safe accepting the ride.

"They stopped at the entrance to Campbell Town for a quick meal; the petrol station there was about the only place along the whole Midland Highway where you could *get* a meal in those days. The driver went for a piss in the shed outside, where a bloke approached saying he was looking for a lift 'north'. He also said he'd noticed the girl and he suggested to the driver that they could each have their way with her.

"This bloke told the driver that on the way out of Campbell Town they should take the road towards Valleyfield. It was dark now and the stranger reckoned the girl wouldn't notice they'd turned off the highway until it was 'too late'.

"The three of them got in the car, the girl now sitting in the back seat, and off they went. The driver turned onto Macquarie Road, which leads to Valleyfield Road and soon they were out of town. It was dark – no houses. The girl couldn't quite hear what the two men in front were saying, but her suspicions were raised by the tone of their talking. She demanded the driver turn around and head back into town. That's when the stranger turned nasty and told the driver to keep going.

"The girl became hysterical, punching both men from behind. The driver stopped. The girl got out, but the stranger was quicker and he grabbed her. She fought, but he punched her in the head. One punch! It killed her. By that time, the driver had come to their side of the car and he panicked. He was furious. The stranger dragged the girl into the ditch and then told the driver to get back in the car and drive away.

"They re-entered the Midland Highway at Epping Forest and drove north in silence. At Perth, the stranger said he'd get out. The driver guessed the bloke was heading for the Devonport Ferry Terminal. "Good riddance!" he thought."

"Do you have any proof for your theory, or is it just an invention on your part?"

Mick countered somewhat obliquely, "that's as good as any other theory, I reckon."

"*Mmm!* That's what you say. Brian, you said you had found extra information – two key pieces of the puzzle – so what are these?"

"Since the time when the police first worked on the case, the science of DNA analysis has made huge gains. Two years ago, the police re-opened what had become a 'cold case' and had some success. The girl had scraps of somebody's skin under her fingernails and luckily those who performed the autopsy had retained this material. *Now*, it was possible to get a good reading of its DNA.

"The result showed that she had fought against a known criminal from New South Wales. His DNA was already on file there and it matched what Tassie's cops now had. They had a name, but unfortunately the bloke was no longer alive. He'd had his head blown off in a Western Sydney gang war four years after he murdered the girl."

"Our police didn't make any of this public, did they?"

"That's right, because – like Mick – *they* thought there were two men involved and they were still searching for the missing one."

"Then, how did you get to know?"

"Only six days ago, I found out about the second piece of the puzzle, when the police quietly let it be known that they now knew there was *no* second man. There was a second person involved, but it was a woman! I now knew the answer to the whole mystery and that's why I raised the subject here today, and also why I jumped on Mick when he said he'd solved it five years ago. He *couldn't* have, and his theory was wrong!"

"What do you mean by 'quietly'?"

"My sister is married to a policeman. After I'd found what I could about the Valleyfield murder, I rang Sis to ask if her hubby ever talked about it. She said he had and she'd ask if he'd talk to me about it as well. He rang a day or two later. I said I'd read what I could find in the newspapers, then he said he'd talk to me only if it was face-to-face, just the two of us. I met him two days ago.

"He explained that, two years ago, when the police learnt the murderer's name, and that he was dead, they confided with the girl's parents. Did they want the public to know? There seemed little to gain – it was pointless to put him on trial! Her parents felt a renewed public exposure was better avoided and they were content in knowing who he was. This was closure for them.

"As I said before, the police didn't want to go public either, while they used this new information to investigate if the murderer had an accomplice who could be prosecuted – if they could find him, of course.

"The detectives began revisiting the Hobart pubs and other places the girl had frequented, this time armed with photos of the murderer that the Sydney police had provided. Six years had passed since she was murdered, so it took a while to trace many of the barmen who'd been there at that time. A couple of them thought they recognised the face, but couldn't recall if he'd had a mate with him.

"The Sydney police were also quizzed. In general, they said the murdered man worked alone. Then, one day, a former Sydney policeman rang Hobart and asked for the detective leading the case. He told the detective that he'd retired only a few months after that gang war in Western Sydney, but he'd had a few occasions in his job to find and talk to the criminal, who was a loner – no criminal mates at least.

"He then told the detective that he'd attended the scene when the criminal's body was found. There'd been a girl there who was hysterical and making a nuisance. The policeman had forcibly removed her from the scene, her photograph had been taken and a squad car took her to where she said she lived.

"A day or two later, the policeman said, he went to this girl's place to find out what she knew about the reason for the gang war. A resident told him the girl had hightailed it out of Sydney, seemingly scared of the gang coming after her.

"He told the detective that he would contact the Sydney police department where this girl's photo would be on file and have it sent to Hobart. He ended by saying to the detective that the girl had a quite unusual face."

"Mick," I said, "it's your shout. I reckon Brian has earned another beer; his throat's parched."

When Mick came back with three beers, Brian continued.

"My brother-in-law said the Tasmanian detectives took the photo around Hobart and also sent it to the police in other states. Apparently it was a dramatic photo – anyone who saw this girl would be very likely to recognise her in the photo.

"This time, two barmen said they'd seen her and one of them thought she had appeared with the murderer – that is, after the detective had produced the criminal's photo.

"All well and good, you could say, but this isn't the end. Several months later, the detective took a phone call from the Kalgoorlie Police. A constable there knew the girl had been in that town for at least a year. She hadn't been in any trouble as far as the police knew; it was the photo that brought the constable to tell his superiors.

"The detective went to talk with the Police Commissioner. It seemed very unlikely that she could be prosecuted for the murder, or even for being an accomplice. It would be easy for her to claim she was an unwilling witness. On that basis, the Commissioner reasoned he'd be accused by the State's Treasurer of wasting public money on a frivolous travel account for a detective to go to Kalgoorlie to interview this girl, but he said he had an idea.

"A notice was distributed to all police in Tasmania, advising that if any member of the force was planning on taking annual leave and intended to visit Western Australia, the Commissioner would like to ask a favour. Two days later, the Commissioner was pleased to tell the detective to contact a female constable and suggest that she consider spending a couple of days in Kalgoorlie. The Department could not pay for the whole cost of getting there, but the cost of varying her planned journey to include Kalgoorlie would be recompensed and whatever time she spent on the diversion could be added to her leave days.

"The constable was given the background and she seemed excited to be of direct service to the Commissioner. She filed a report six weeks later, to the effect that the girl *denied* being in Tasmania with the criminal, but the girl said he had told her during the time she spent with him in Sydney that he had been to Tassie; that he stole a car in Hobart to return to Devonport for the ferry, and on the way he'd picked up a girl – thinking he'd be able to have sex along the way. He'd tried, but she fought like a tiger and he'd lost his cool, punched her – too well, unfortunately."

Brian ended with, "most criminals have a short fuse and don't care for anyone other than themselves. The girl's story made sense."

I turned to Mick. "Next time anyone says they've a story to tell, sit and listen to the story!"

TREFOIL ISLAND
And the Short-Tailed Shearwater
Graeme Bourke

I arrived at Wynyard airport at ten in the morning, it was a magnificent clear sunny day with the wind blowing quite strongly from the south west. I was flying to Trefoil Island which is situated off the north west tip of Tasmania near Cape Grim. It is part of the Trefoil Island Group and is owned by the Trefoil Island Aboriginal Cooperative. Access is by plane or by boat on the eastern shore at a pebbly beach. Most of the island has sheer cliffs.

The reason for my trip to the island was to connect up a new back-up generator for the processing and freezing of mutton birds and associated amenity buildings. The Short-Tailed Shearwater, or Tasmanian mutton bird, breeds in the tens of millions on the islands stretching from Recherche Arch in Western Australia, through to South Australia, Victoria and the Bass Strait islands. It returns to Australia from its summer feeding waters near Japan in the northern hemisphere around October to lay its single egg in burrows underneath the stringy tussocks and on the sloping banks.

It was estimated that there are around three million birds on Trefoil alone, so burrows are always at a premium. Many birds lay their eggs on the ground where they are quickly taken by snakes, seagulls and all the other birds of prey that frequent the area. It is a time of plenty for nature.

The bird is a smoky brown colour, with a paler throat and silky gloss on the underwings. They travel in immense flocks, passing in undulating streams and becoming churning masses on the sea when feeding. They rest on the surface of the water in dark rafts. I was lucky enough to witness this sight one evening to the west of Trefoil.

The plane soared off into the air and as it reached a height of two and a half thousand feet, I began taking photos, one of which I entered into a local calendar competition and it was duly selected as one of the winners. I have never failed to be surprised at the beauty of this island state of Tasmania.

Flying past Robbins Island, just off Smithton brings back memories from long ago when I used to collect the mutton bird myself as a young man. Every March we would make the journey by plane, usually flown by local identity Bill Vincent from the Smithton airport. Robbins is an indistinct mostly flat low-lying island. The only real area of height is on the western tip where the mutton bird rookery is situated.

We used to camp under the lea of the hill and little good it did us when the storms came through, as strong winds are notorious in Bass Strait. One time we spent the night in an old dairy huddling in the corners and pulling anything we could over the top of us. As I recall, we used plastic sheeting and old galvanised iron as the wind whipped the heavy rain through every crack and joint in the building. Our windblown, wet and soggy tents were forgotten as we listened to the ferocious whistling of the wind. The wind gods had gone crazy, so it seemed.

Flying over Woolnorth Point, which is the true north-west corner of Tasmania, I could see Trefoil Island up ahead. Its light brown surface indicated a layer of button grass atop a rocky formation of dark grey cliffs that dominated the south, the east and the northern sides of the island. A sloping bank with a winding track could be clearly seen on the western side which led to a hut not far from the shore. This was the bottom camp.

The pilot banked the plane as he circled for the approach, the Doughboy Islands, looking like two loaves of bread and Cape Grim were visible to the south. Cape Grim has a weather station which monitors the purest air in the world. Straightening up the pilot steered the Cessna down onto the strip with a couple subtle bumps, before taxying the plane towards the main buildings.

The first thing I had to do was check out the generator and make sure that it would still run as it had hit the ground when being carried onto the island by the helicopter. Some of the wiring had been jarred loose, the radiator was bent and damaged, and the fan was split. The battery was damaged beyond repair. Still, we were able to test run the generator and make sure that it was still working; we would have to order some new parts and make the repairs later.

I settled down to some dinner with the other workers, some of whom I already knew. For lunch we had saveloys and mashed potatoes, there was plenty to go around. I even went back for seconds having not had anything to eat since early morning. In the afternoon I concentrated on getting the new mains to the generator through the conduits from one building to the other and reburied into the ground. At five o'clock we stopped work and had a few drinks of cold beer. It had been a very hot and windy day, one had to continually hold onto one's hat, as the strong wind would often lift it from your head and blow it away. Having been introduced to the other workers during the day, I enjoyed these few moments after work to relax.

I was billeted in what they called the top camp, a low-lying shack with a combined dining room and kitchen. It had three bedrooms and I was lucky enough to have a room to myself. I was sharing the hut with Paul and Danny. The bathroom was rather basic; a bucket on a rope was the shower and a concrete lintel the floor. After boiling some hot water on the gas stove I filled the bucket up and enjoyed a short sharp shower. Dinner was in the main camp that night. That evening I sat out in front of the shack sheltered from the buffeting Roaring Forties and marvelled at the view. Languishing there in the peace and quiet, the sun, the land and the sea took on a golden hue. The dry grass in front of me rippled and wavered as if under siege by a tempest.

The waves in the sea were capped with white as the wind drove the tops into the air forcing out a white stream that looked like a giant spider web as the water thundered over the reefs and small islands in the bay. In the distance I could see the low silhouette of Hunter Island, looking rustic in the evening light. The horizon seemed to blend with the sea making it hard to distinguish the end of the sea and the beginning of the sky.

As darkness crept over the land the first mutton birds began to appear. Their wings beating fast as they climbed into the air above the cliffs and then proceeded to gently glide across the button grass as they searched for their burrows. It never ceases to amaze me how the birds find their particular burrow amongst the thousands upon thousands on the island. There are no streets, no numbers here, just a basic homing instinct that has seen these birds breed and multiply over thousands of years.

The chicks in the burrows will move towards the entrance and begin their shrieking cry to attract the adult birds that have been at sea all day gathering food. One of the things that I notice almost immediately is the strong distinctive smell of the mutton bird as more and more gather in the sky. It is hard to describe the smell to someone who has never been on a mutton bird rookery. The scent of feathers come to mind with a pungent, stale and tangy odour.

On finding the burrow the adult bird will be greeted by even more shrieks as the chick makes its demand for food. The meal is regurgitated from the adult bird and is an evil smelling green oily mixture that the chick devours eagerly.

The amount of birds in the air becomes thicker and thicker, until the sky is almost blotted out. How they manage to avoid each other and the buildings on the island also amazes me. Even so, during the night I occasionally heard the thud of a bird hitting the tin roof, then a scurry and scratching of flapping wings as they try to gain their feet on the slippery surface.

By this time all the workers have returned to their respective huts, thus reducing the danger of vehicles running over the many mutton birds that are now beginning to congregate on the ground and blocking the tracks. In the darkness the island takes on a whole new dimension, the ground beneath your very feet seems to come alive. You can sense the vibrations, the pulsing and throbbing of life itself.

By the time I rise the next morning there isn't a mutton bird in sight and it is very quiet. Breakfast consisted of some tinned fruit. The wind is not as strong today; even so it is still warm. I concentrated on getting the mains through the roof of the main building using a couple of lengths of conduit. Lunch consisted of salad and ham, of which I went back for seconds again. This island life was making me hungry. I completed the mains run to the switchboard and to the generator and began wiring up the generator light and power.

Finishing work at five, and after a few cans of beer, we had some cottage pie for dinner. After, we went down to the bottom camp to meet some other workers who were coming over in a boat from Woolnorth Point with more supplies.

On Trefoil there is no jetty, no beach to bring the boats in on, and no natural harbour. The boats have to be towed up onto black rubble-strewn embankment with a strong rope attached to a tractor. To launch the boats, it is all hands on deck as the aluminium boats are turned on the rubble and pushed down in the sea.

As we made our way back up the dusty track on the four-wheel motorbike in the darkness, thousands of birds flew around us missing us by mere feet. Many were landing and now posed a threat on the trail. We managed to negotiate our way through the chaos without running over any birds.

The next day I had a bit of time to myself as I was waiting for some lining to go on in the building so I took a stroll down to a cairn that sat on the edge of the airstrip. It seems Trefoil is not without its tragedy. In March of 2003 a Cessna crashed on take-off killing the pilot and three passengers. Also, back in 1895 Albert Kay ran sheep on the island and on returning from the island in a small flat-bottom boat, Albert and two of his children, Walter who was sixteen and Sara of four years were drowned.

His wife Maria had watched the tragedy unfold from the shore with Robert of twenty two months in her arms. He had narrowly escaped drowning as well when Maria took him from the boat. Under the guidance of Belinda, the eldest girl, her mother and five siblings survived unassisted on the island for six weeks before they were rescued.

I had completed all my work as far as I could go. I was still waiting for some of the plaster sheet to go on, so I had a leisurely day, although with some excitement. A snake catcher had flown in and was scouring the area for specimens. After an hour or two he returned with a couple of large tiger snakes. The snakes here survive by eating their fill when the mutton birds arrive, they eat the young and the eggs. Then they have to wait for a year before they can feed again.

That evening dinner was in the top camp with roast beef, pork and chicken on the menu along with pumpkin peas and gravy, a sumptuous meal of huge proportions. The visitors from Friday were returning to Woolnorth Point with the boat and some gear the next day. I was to go back with them after agreeing to drive two of them back home to Burnie as they wanted to have a few beers.

We loaded up the boat and headed out across the bay into a stiff north westerly that had the waves crashing over the bow of the boat. As I sat in the boat looking back at the island, I could not help but think about Robert Kay rowing out into this dangerous stretch of water in a small flat-bottom boat with his two children and his wife standing on the shore with six of her children. It reminded me of my only family tragedy when six of my grandmother's siblings were drowned in the 1929 floods.

MY COUSIN ANNIE
or
THE SKELTONS IN MY UNCLE'S CUPBOARD
Ant Dry

The Last time I saw my cousin Annie, she was ten and I seventeen. She had no siblings and I, the youngest of three boys had always hankered after a baby sister, so we hit it off very well. I spent hours pandering to her every need. I'd push her on the swings, read her stories, watch cartoons with her and have long rambling talks on all matters girlie. Perhaps that was a bit odd. Perhaps I was a peculiar teenager, but that was the way it was. I loved my cousin unreservedly.

We lived a thousand kilometers apart, so our meetings were annual affairs, held every April and only because our grandmother would take the pilgrimage North from Cape Town to stay with my Uncles Brian, Len and Mark in Johannesburg and we would travel down from Salisbury to do the same. The trip was always in April as that was the one time that my grandmother was happy to go to Johannesburg. She was very frightened by thunder, and April was the one time of the year when it was guaranteed there would be no thunder storms.

My father and his three brothers had had a curious upbringing. Len and Brian had been brought up speaking Afrikaans and Mark and my Father had been brought up speaking English. In retrospect it was curious that I never asked why this was the case, but South Africa was a difficult place in which to live, and it was best not to ask too many questions. Back in the1930s and 40s when my father was growing up the hatred between the two white "tribes" as it were, was palpable and perhaps my grandfather thought he could unite the tribes by his sons being members of both. I don't know. Probably not. My grandfather was a shit, and I doubt he had such pure motives. More likely he knew it would lead to conflict and relished the idea.

Almost by design, the boys grew up distrusting each other. The Afrikaans speakers were encouraged to do "manly" things, play rugby and the like. The English speakers were allowed to get on with their schoolwork. They drifted apart and snarled at each other over the dinner table.

Distrust lead to secrets. Brian never told anyone what he was up to. No one was really sure what he did for a living. He moved away from home and made a lot of money very quickly. My father was vague about how Brian made his money, as he did not know himself, but he thought it had something to so with gambling and the stock market. Dad told stories how Brian would play cards and would put his head on the table to see what the dealer was giving to the other players. Brian was too quick with his fists for anyone to object more than once. Brian bought a fancy house and drove a Mercedes Benz.

It was my relationship with Annie that re-united my father and my Uncle Brian for a while. They were both surprised at how well we got on. My father was amused, my Uncle relieved to have a free baby-sitter for two weeks of the year.

Slowly the rift between the brothers grew less wide.

The year I turned 18 I was called up to do my National Service, so for the first time in many years I didn't get to see Annie. She wrote to me instead, long rambling missives peppered with drawings and stories of her various animals and what they were all up to. Generally, the letters would be accompanied by a bar of chocolate as she knew my weaknesses and assumed there was a shortage.

My grandmother died while I was on National Service. My father flew down for the funeral, and something happened when the four brothers were together. I never got the full story, but it caused the final rift between the two sets of brothers. The actual set-to had something to do with a piano and a TV set. I think my father was enraged that Brian descended on Granny's house and loaded the TV, the piano and the books into his car. He felt that Brian should have shown a bit more respect to the dead. "She was not even cold in her grave, and he was stripping her house bare" was his complaint. There may have been more to it than that. I never found out. What it showed was that the old conflict had never died. Perhaps the final fallout was bound to happen.

I thought I'd never see Annie again.

I went to university and got on with my life. I never travelled to Johannesburg, so never had cause to seek her out. I doubt that my Uncle Brian would have been very welcoming anyway. I assumed Annie went to school, grew up and forgot that she had ever had a big cousin.

My memory of our time together assumed rose tinted hues - as is natural I suppose. I remembered her with fondness, and as the time grew, became accustomed to the idea that I would never see her again. I thought it best too, as no doubt after all that time the relationship would never be the same. Things would have changed and we would have disappointed each other.

Annie became a fond if somewhat dim and distant memory.

****

Two weeks ago, I was introduced to facebook messenger. Our gym group needed a way of communicating, so one of the more tech savvy members set us up as a group for messaging purposes. I'd had facebook for years, but never been more than a reader of posts. Now, because I was a member of a group, I had a play with messenger, which I'd not even known existed. I saw that I had a message, dated two years previous from someone called Ann Terry.

The message asked: "Are you the son of Alec Dry from Riversdale? Regards Ann(Dry)"

It was my cousin Annie. Forty years on.

We reconnected and it was wonderful. The years fell away as if we had seen each other only last year. We Skyped and talked for two hours the first time, longer the next. She lives in New Zealand now and we have plans to get together soon.

She told me that some five years previous to our reconnection, she had received a phone call from a woman called Marjorie Sellman, who claimed to be her sister. She had dismissed the caller assuming there was a scam involved, as she knew she had no siblings.

The woman, Marjorie wrote to her next, and enclosed proof that she was indeed Ann's sister, with the same mother and father. She was two years older than Ann. It appeared that her parents had fallen pregnant with Marjorie before they were married. Such was the stigma in South Africa in those days, that they had had to give the child up for adoption.

Annie's mother had died at this stage, and her father had developed Alzheimer's and was living with her. Annie felt she could not confront him with this news, as he was very confused most of the time, so instead, she called her Aunt who was still living in South Africa.

She told her Aunt: "I've just discovered I have a sister. Do you know anything about it?"

Her Aunt replied, "Yes, I've known for years. But it's not a sister, it's a brother."

And so Annie discovered that she had a brother too. Her brother was about a year younger than her. He had been born with Downs Syndrome, and had been rejected by her father, who did not want to carry the stigma of fathering a "deformed" child. Brian's mother in law had refused to accept the rejection and had collected the child from the home into which his parents had placed him, and she had brought him up as her own.

Annie had met her brother many times, but had been lead to believed that he was her Uncle.

All through this journey of discovery Annie had her father living with her. Not even in his moments of clarity did she bring the matter up with him, as he had a foul temper and she believed that he had probably expunged his two other children from his memory anyway.

Marjory asked to meet her father. After some thought, Annie agreed but on the understanding that Brian would not be told who she was.

They duly met and Annie says that Brian would look at Marjory intently on a regular basis. Perhaps some memory was stirred as Marjory did bear some resemblance to her mother.

Marjory was true to her word and never mentioned to Brian who she was, but on the last night she was there, Brian's carer blurted out the truth to Brian. It was as if nothing had been said. Brian did not react at all, but the next day when Marjory left and came to say goodbye, Brian stood up, hugged her and kissed her goodbye, something he had never done to anyone before.

One has to wonder what other skeletons we shall find in my Uncle's cupboard.

ONE SMALL WORLD
Jennie Herrera

Those first photographs from space:
it's hard to remember the way we oohhed and aahhed
as we gazed on them; like first glance in a traded mirror.
Not reflections in a pond. They were too precise.

We hung, we whirled, we looked so plump and round and blue.
We looked so beautiful.
                    So perfect.
                    So alone.
They started then:
An Ark. Spaceship Earth. An adventurous sound about it,
yet a homely sense of comfort. And we didn't say soon enough:

                    So small.
                    So limited.

For our ambitions. All contained within that spinning ball,
that little thing that might hang and jig upon a Christmas tree,
bright,
shining, insouciant, its snow inside a paperweight. And from it
we ask everything. But never give it what other beings offer:

hibernation, a resting space, a time when it might sleep and recuper-
ate.

When it dies it will die from lack of sleep.

*

The first time it appeared on screens, the first time it was shown in
books,
we didn't stop to ask what we'd done to deserve a planet in its spinning glory.
We didn't stop …
We took it as our due.

We didn't stop to give it love and care.
We didn't stop to let it sleep.
We whirled. It whirled.
We thought that people smart enough to hurl into space,
to cut their earth-bound fetters, had cut their links to cause and
effect,
       life and death; had no need to finger chains, called the
sceptics
          crude names, said 'where's your sense of adventure?'
More now than mere world, this luscious aphrodisiac world
was our oyster. We ordered a dozen, then a dozen more,
        to tip and slide between lip and taste

SPRING
Lesley Podmore - 2011

Bright blossoms flourish,
My garden's alive,
Torrential rain doesn't bother,
They all seem to thrive,
Sweet petals a-falling,
Cascading around,
There's carpets of orange all over the ground.
        "Nanna , come look", my grand-daughters say,
        "Crunchy-Nut Cornflakes for fairies today".

THE PAINTING'S REPLY
Brenda Slavoff

I didn't want to have my likeness
taken, this of all days, when I'd
been up all night with the toothache
(and had the blasted thing out
in the morning, oh miserie! - the barber
hauled out of his bed at cock crow.)
But you know the temperamental artist,
It's got to be *this* day:
"No, donna, it cannot be next week,
I have a commission to paint a fresco..."
as if *I* haven't lots to do, what with
Easter approaching and my cook just dropped
dead of the plague; "...a religious work,
and I plan a new method of application,
so I can go over it again and again..."
Well, I tried that with my lead powder, and
couldn't cover the red swelling of my jaw -
"...until it is perfect. As your picture
will be, one day." Well, that day
never came, as it turned out; the
temperamental artist absconded
with the promised result, and it was
found in his possession at
his death. But you know
how men are; they range themselves
against women, even when they have
nothing to gain. "He'll cover up
the swollen jaw; don't worry so much
about the way you look," even though
it was going to be on the wall
for all posterity to see. Grandchildren
will cry out, "There's Grandmama!"
My daughter-in-law, a stiff-necked
upstart with a dowry, will snigger at my face
though *she*'s no beauty. "Oh Lisa," my husband

protested, "don't make a fuss.
The artist can only do the painting
this week. I've paid the deposit
already." Ill-graced, in pain, I posed
for that mountebank, that
swindler, who took off with
the deposit and never delivered
the "perfect" portrait. Holy saints,
what's to be our reward in Heaven
for such ungodly dishonesty?

AN EVENING WITH BEN MILBOURNE
Ant Dry

From the Website of Ghost Rock Vineyard: *Ghost Rock Vineyard, situated 10 minutes east of Devonport on Tasmania's Central North Coast, offers a modern cellar door experience. You can taste, enjoy and purchase our wines including our famous Tasmanian Pinot Chardonnay Sparkling (Catherine). We also produce Pinot Noir, Sauvignon Blanc, Pinot Gris, Chardonnay, Riesling and pinot Rose. Owners Cate and Colin Arnold invite you to visit and sample their award winning Tasmanian wines while taking in the tranquil vineyard and countryside views to Bass Strait*
From the Website of Ben Milbourne: *Ben was a contestant in reality TV show "Masterchef". Born and living still in Devonport, North West Tasmania, Ben is incredibly passionate about what he does - he doesn't do his job for the pay check. The outdoors inspires him and living in Tasmania allows him to make the most of this. His strengths in cooking are in Mexican and Asian cooking.*

My wife is a great fan of reality TV shows, so when she saw that Ben Milbourne was offering a series of Private Dinners at Ghost Rock it was a no brainer for her to buy tickets to the inaugural dinner.

We invited my brother Dave and his wife to join us, and off we traipsed.

Ghost Rock Winery has a splendid setting in the rolling hills east of Devonport, but this was not shown to its best advantage when we arrived, as being winter, it was pitch dark! Despite this the gardens in front of the cellar door were lit and the entrance was warmly inviting and impressive.

The reception/dining area is not large, and the two tables which seated a total of 24 diners, filled the entire space. It was a beautiful sight. The linen was crisp and clean, the cutlery was resplendent shiny and plentiful, and the glasses twinkled everywhere.

We were offered a glass of bubbly on arrival and soon after were asked to take our seats.

The owner of Ghost Rock, Colin Arnold began proceedings by welcoming us to the inaugural event. He told us that along with the five courses we would be indulging in we would be treated to a number of pinot noirs from the vineyard. The first pinot was from his Clarendon estate and was a 2008 vintage. We were each poured a liberal portion into the largest of the glasses in front of us. The glass was about the size of a football, so the portion given to us seemed quite small, although I was struck by how long it took the vintner to pour such a small amount.

Ben himself them came out of the kitchen and told us a bit about the courses we would be partaking in throughout the evening. We were told that all recipes would be available in his book which was to be published on 1 November, which he irrelevantly informed us was co-incidentally also Mexican Independence Day.

Our first course was "Hot smoked salmon with puffed wild rice, beetroot crème fraiche and spiced sourdough crumb". The salmon, pink and innocent was arranged in a semi-circle around the edge of the plate, very artistically presented, almost too pretty to eat. It was superb, with an exquisite array of flavours and textures. Had the plate carried three times as much as it did, I would have happily wolfed it down, but thank goodness it did not, as I still had four courses to go!

Our wine glasses were topped up steadily.

The second course was "Duck and lychee curry with red basmati and picked salad". I had raved about the first course and this one was just as good. The duck may have been just slightly tough, but the flavour combinations and the differing textures of the food and the arrangement of colours more than made up for this.

To accompany the second course, we were given the 2012 Pinot Noir which had won an international award. It came from the "Two Blocks" estate. I was surprised to see that I had finished the wine I had been served for the first course and felt very ready for more.

The third course was "Lamb backstrap with ancient grain salad and chipotle spiced yoghurt". I have always loved lamb, and this was an ode to lamb, beautifully cooked, wonderfully spiced and fully flavoursome. The 'ancient grain salad' comprised a mixture of wild rice, Israeli couscous, chickpeas, quinoa, pomegranate seeds, barbaries, lemon juice orange juice and olive oil. 'Chipotle' is a smoked chilli. The flavour range sent my taste buds on a dance of joy.

This course was served with the 2009 Pinot Noir from the Clairedown Estate.

I had an epiphany during this third course, namely that the vineyard had made too much pinot noir and that they were using us to get rid of it for them. Every time I took a sip, my wine glass was filled.

During this course, my brother and I became engaged in conversation with one of the other guests who it would appear was about to embark on a trip to Geneva to address the United Nations on inter-celestial bodies, whatever they are. His name was George, and he was a PhD in something, I forget what. My brother pulled out his mobile telephone, googled a number of PhD jokes and entertained George. George smiled.

The fourth course was a bit of a blur. According to the menu, it was "Slow roasted brisket with smashed potatoes, braised shallots and blistered truss tomatoes". Ben came out of the kitchen again and the only things I remember with clarity that he said were that brisket was coming back into fashion and that he had smashed the potatoes with the palm of his hand. I may, of course be mistaken. This course was pretty good too.

The wine was a "Mystery wine' and we were ask to guess what it may be. My brother loudly suggested diet coke, which did not make the vintner smile. Since it was a pinot noir evening that was pretty easy, so I duly responded, only to have it suggested that we were being asked to tell from which part of the winery the crop came. No one had a clue. We were told that the wine had "a bit of a nose" and that it "drank like a merlot", whatever that all means. Eventually it was revealed that it came from Claim 115, wherever that was. All I know is that it tasted good and went down very easily.

At this stage, my brother's jokes were becoming very confused and confusing, but we all laughed none the less. George offered to sing us a song, but his wife quickly put a stop to that.

I only remember bits of the final course, which was "Modern apple crumble with poached rhubarb, crème anglaise and praline crumb". My wife tells me that it was exquisite and that I had told her repeatedly that I had thought it was the best desert I had ever eaten. Whatever.

As we left, having bought three bottles of the mystery wine, we noticed that most of the other diners had organised transport home. Very sensible. Thankfully my wife had nominated herself Des for the evening so we were Okay. Conversation lagged a bit on the way home, so I looked over to the back seat to find my brother and his wife asleep with their heads on each other shoulders. A fitting end to a wonderful evening.

THE FAIRY QUEEN'S WISH
Dawn Meredith

In a hidden, sunlit glade in The Secret Wood, there once lived an old Fairy Queen. Every leaf, toadstool and flower glittered with her fairy dust, which was almost invisible to the human eye.

The Fairy Queen sat upon her pansy throne of deepest purple velvet and felt sad. Her husband had died and she was very old herself. She had lived a long and healthy life, adored by the fairies of Secret Wood, but she had no daughter to take over as queen. Only fairy queens ruled in Secret Wood and to her great sadness she had no children at all.

The Fairy Queen had twinkling blue eyes and a delicate long nose on which she perched her pink glasses, so that she could see better. Her wavy silver hair flowed all the way down her back and was tended to by a team of hair-do fairies, who delighted in combing and arranging tiny flowers in it. The Fairy Queen had fine porcelain skin, with hardly a wrinkle, despite her great age of six hundred and forty six years.

But no matter her beauty, she had no heir and her kingdom was doomed to be taken over by the Goblin King, who regularly buzzed in to visit and pester her with questions.

The Goblin King was short and ugly, with a new wart on his face every week. His hair was tatty and green and he wore the same dirty waistcoat every day. He had no manners, the goblin king, but even though she detested his bad breath and poor personal habits, the Fairy Queen was unfailingly polite to her rival. All the fairies had been instructed not to speak to him, for fear they would anger him and be drawn into a war. This the Fairy Queen did not want, especially at her advanced age. "It is better to appear a fool and stay silent, than to open one's mouth and prove it," she had insisted. The Fairy Queen was both dignified and wise.

The Goblin King was insufferable, but he, too, had a burden. He was in love with the Fairy Queen; had been for the last three hundred or so years. Being a goblin, of course, he was expected to choose a goblin wife, but no one in his kingdom could match the Fairy Queen for beauty, elegance, refinement and kindness, so he remained unmarried. Of course, he realised she must loathe him and his goblin ways, but he knew no better. Because there was no other leader, he would come to rule after the Fairy Queen and he wanted to rule as wisely as she, so he pestered her with questions.

The Fairy Queen noticed that the Goblin King seemed to have a sense of responsibility for her kingdom, but there was always that tiny glint in his eye that she did not quite trust. Was it greed? She couldn't be sure. Her heart felt even sadder at this, for he would probably outlive her, being a hundred years younger. Her fairy kingdom was doomed. There was no fairy baby.

Then, one day, an old, wounded badger stumbled into the glade. His black and white fur was bloodied and smelled of decay. Despite his injuries, he caused a panic among the fairies, who scattered in fright to hide. However, the Fairy Queen, typically compassionate, sent her best physicians to tend to the old badger's wounds.

Word was sent back to the Fairy Queen that the badger had a message, for her ears only. The Fairy Queen was mystified. What could a dying badger have to say to the Queen of the Fairies? She flew, surrounded by her attendants, to alight down softly at his head, for he was a much larger creature than she. The badger's eyes were yellowed and ill, saliva drooled out of his mouth and his front paws were damaged beyond repair.

The Fairy Queen's soft heart felt sorry for the badger. It had obviously travelled far and fought off many enemies. She sent her fairies away and approached the badger carefully. "Dear badger, how may I help you?" she asked.

The badger looked up at the beautiful, elderly Fairy Queen and gasped. Her silver hair was backlit by the sun and her face shone like moonbeams. Her eyes sparkled with warmth and kindness. He swallowed and gathered his strength.

"Fair queen, I see the legends of your beauty and kindness are true, for you have sent your best physicians to tend to me. Alas, I am dying, but not before I give you this message. Do not abandon hope for a child. One shall be given to you, of fairy blood." The badger paused to cough weakly. "Prepare a feast of celebration, for if you believe in these words, your dearest wish will come true."

The Fairy Queen had so many questions. She touched the badger's battered face gently and said, "Dear badger, please tell me, how could this happen? I am old, with few years left myself, and the Goblin King would take my throne and govern my kingdom. I have little choice but to let him."

The badger took a long, shallow breath which whistled out through his nose. His chest heaved with the effort. The Fairy Queen could sense his heartbeat slowing and feared she would not discover the whole of his story before he passed away.

"Fair queen, I come as messenger from the King of the Realm. He has seen your plight and granted you this one wish, but you must truly believe, or it shall not come to pass."

The Fairy Queen had never heard of the King of the Realm. Was he a fairy too? Perhaps a goblin, or worse, a troll?

"Dearest badger, please tell me, who is the King of the Realm? What sort of creature will he send me to rule my kingdom after I am gone? I am afraid to accept his kind offer."

The badger rolled his eyes restlessly. "Fair queen, The King of the Realm sent me in secret to give this message to you. He sees the Goblin King's desire to govern your kingdom and fears the de-mise of all fair folk, should a goblin rule them. This, surely, you have also considered?"

The Fairy Queen trembled with fear, for, yes, she had indeed thought about the future of her folk, should the Goblin King come to rule in her stead. He seemed almost kind in his attentions, but what would happen once she lay cold in the earth? He may become an evil tyrant. Perhaps the only option she had was to trust this King of the Realm, this unknown figure, who had sent a secret messenger.

"Dear, dear badger, how can I know this to be the truth, that an unknown King of the Realm is able to grant such a wish?"

The badger sighed. He had only a moment or two left to deliver his message. His breath was fainter, his heartbeats slow and erratic.

"Fair queen, there is no guarantee that would please you. This is the nature of belief, in things which cannot be seen or proven. I can only say this, that I was once a fairy myself…" He paused, wincing in pain. The Fairy Queen clasped her hands in delight and her eyes shone with tears.

"You were once a fairy?" She touched his matted fur lovingly and stroked his face.

"Yes. I travelled far beyond the fairy kingdom, to the Realm of which I now speak. There I met the King of the Realm as a young-ster, who had followed his father's hunting expedition. His horse had thrown him off at a hedgerow and he lay badly wounded. I flew to the palace for help and in so doing saved his life. For this act I received one wish from his father, the old King of the Realm. My wish was to travel beyond all the known kingdoms, as a strong and independent creature of day or night. Thus you see before you the creature's body he gave me - a badger's."

"Dearest badger, such a tale you tell! But how can this help me in my dire hour?" said the Fairy Queen in distress.

"My time has finally come," said the badger feebly. "But this I say to you - believe, fair queen, and it shall come to pass! Your wish for a child to rule in your place shall be granted. As I was granted one wish, so shall you, for your kindness and tolerance, be also granted a wish. Farewell… great beauty… of Fairydom."

The badger closed his eyes and as she watched his last breath sigh out of his body, the Fairy Queen saw it gather as a mist, swirling and turning, growing thicker. A tiny form began to take shape in the air. The sunlight broke through the trees at that very moment and sparkled with magic light upon the shifting shape. The Fairy Queen stood, her arms ready, her eyes alight with love. The shimmering light faded and there, in her arms, was a fairy baby, a girl, with white-gold hair and the palest blue eyes she had ever seen. The baby cried and snuggled into the old queen's breast.

The Fairy Queen called for her attendants. She laid the child upon the softest petal cradle and called for some milk. Then she prepared a feast of celebration. Joy spread like a fire throughout the kingdom and the fairy folk came to pay their respects to the Fairy Queen's child. They were awed by her white-gold hair and palest of blue eyes. A miracle had occurred!

The Fairy Queen lived a further sixteen years, long enough to train her daughter, Cilla, in the ways of wise rulership. And when the old queen finally closed her eyes in eternal sleep, Cilla buried her alongside the King, who had lain waiting these many long decades. Even the Goblin King paid his respects and then left, never to return again.

Cilla, the young, white-haired Fairy Queen, ruled as wisely as her mother and was beloved by all. In time she married and bore five daughters and three sons.

The fairy kingdom continues to this day, in the sunlit, hidden glade, where every leaf, toadstool and flower glitters with fairy dust, almost invisible to the human eye. If you believe.

CHRISTMAS IN THREE LANDS
Dawn Meredith

When I was little, Christmases in England were crisp and cool, with snow, red woollen tights and a fluffy white hat that covered your ears. I tottered towards my grandmother's open arms in my little fur-lined boots. Carolers went from door to door singing all our favourite Christmas carols. In the mornings there would be either snow or crunchy frost on the ground and frozen puddles you could skid on. We had enormous hot dinners with roast lamb, baked vegetables, mint sauce and gravy and Yorkshire pudding. Hot custard was dribbled over rich Christmas pud, bursting with glace cherries and cinnamon. We lived near the sea, in Eastbourne and I loved to walk along the promenade in all weathers. When the wind pushed me sideways, and sprayed me with flecks of salt water I giggled with delight.

Snug and homey, Christmases in England gathered family around you like a warm cloak.

The next year I had a little sister, who got all the attention, even when I squealed with joy as I unwrapped my presents. But the tinsel had not yet lost its glamour. The fire blazed, the adults swirled their brandy in large round glasses and chatted about past Christmases. The cat snoozed on the sofa, on top of the discarded Christmas wrapping paper, its belly full. It was heaven and I didn't know anything else.

When I was five, it all changed. We sailed on an enormous ship to Australia, arriving in one of the hottest cities – Perth. What would an Australian Christmas be like? No cool, crisp mornings with a smattering of snow. Instead we put white zinc on our noses, grabbed our towels and arm 'floaties' and headed to the beach. The BEACH! Hot sun. beating down relentlessly, sand in your food, your mouth, your ears, your hair. Mum was thrilled she didn't have to bake a roast dinner. No more Yorkshire pudding and delicious gravy for us. Now we scoffed cold meats, seafood and *salad.* Sunburnt, we returned home cranky, with salt encrusted bathers. Even when we stayed home for a 'barbie' with sausages and steaks and swam in the pool, somehow it just wasn't Christmas *at all.*

But luckily, when I was twelve, Christmas returned. At the beginning of December we flew on a plane, my first trip, to Europe, landing in Germany. We were upside down now, as far as the seasons go. It was winter and we'd left the scorching Perth heat behind. Adding to my excitement, we were going to be meeting a whole new family in Norway. Our Norwegian grandfather, *Bestefar,* picked us up in his beautiful European car, with the perfect shiny paintwork, luscious leather seats and oh-so-quiet, purring engine. Our journey was far from over. We would be travelling north, to our new home. Bestefar's car glided along smooth roads, past mountains, charming houses and such green grass! Bare trees lined the streets, lifting their arms to the sky, their feet in dark, moist earth. The air smelled *different.* No eucalyptus and teatree here. It was rich and ancient. The hairs on my arms stood up at the scent on the wind – adventure.

Bestefar chuckled as he asked us questions, interpreted by my step-mother. He was a neat man, with buttoned up shirt, slicked black hair and twinkly blue eyes. I watched as he turned confidently onto the autobahn, where cars flashed past at frightening speeds. We drove through countries in a single day, not like Australia where you experience the same barren landscape for days, crossing the Nullabor Plain, hot winds slashing your face through the open window because the air conditioner has broken down.

"Look!" I squealed, feeling a familiar joy. "Snow!" My sister was too young to remember English Christmases, but they were embedded in my soul's memory. The snugness, the quiet of a snowy garden, the brandy swirling adults sitting by the fire - it all came back at once. Bestefar stopped the car and we got out to run our hands over the freezing white softness.

We crossed the sea to Sweden on a ferry whose bow lifted up to let trucks and cars drive onboard. We drove through great pine *skog,* forest, and across the border into Norway. At the petrol station Bestefar filled up with *bensin* and gave me some change, tiny coins with strange letters; *50 øre, 1 krone.* Soon we were at Bestefar and Bestemor's house, *Fosse Stua,* in Lillehammer. We'd left Perth in forty degree heat. Now it was minus twenty four. What a winter wonderland! The snow was piled so high the roads became white tunnels, where you had to dangle reflectors from your pockets to be seen when out walking at night. My sister and I rode a *spark,* which is basically a wooden chair on steel rails, with a handle bar on the back of the chair. They use them to nip into town for groceries. You stand on the rails behind the chair and kick off, like a scooter. On icy roads they are FAST! I made it my mission to scare my sister to death on sharp turns, downhill, at breathtaking speed, the hairs inside my nose stiff with frost.

A few weeks later we had our first Norwegian Christmas, on an island in Romsdal's fjord, surrounded by a large family who didn't speak English. We were *fremede,* foreigners, in a magnificent land of soaring mountains and deep, icy fjords; of vast green valleys and traditions old as time itself. Bestefar and Bestemor's wooden holiday house, *Solheim,* Sun Home, perched on a hillside beside the red painted barn. A small forest curved protectively behind it and offered glimpses of brave deer and their fawns in early morning light. The sloping lawn give way to a shoreline of grey rocks, worn round by the sea for thousands of years. The ocean's white tips cantered off to the other side of the fjord to pull up abruptly at sheer, dark mountains with snowy caps. A watery path wove up between these rock giants to destinations only the cruise ships knew. When outside, we all wore bright, woollen jumpers, tights under our outer clothing, knitted hats and gloves we'd borrowed from our new cousins.

Christmas Day finally arrived! At Onkel Kjell-Arne's house, *Fjell Ro,* Mountain Peace, a great pile of presents squatted in the middle of the *stua,* loungeroom. And as Onkel Kjell-Arne played Santa, my sister and I marvelled at the number of presents, the crowd surrounding us, the snug feeling of love and acceptance by these people who really were strangers to us. Later, while the adults chatted and drank *Vørter* øl we dressed in layers and ran outside. Laughing, we plonked ourselves upon tiny plastic *akebret,* sleds, and whizzed down the slope to the sea, sometimes three passengers on top of each other, shrieking with laughter. Icicles clung to my fringe and my cheeks tingled. I didn't care that my bottom was wet and my gloves sodden too. Christmas had come to rest in its rightful place in my heart. The richness of a winter Christmas – being indoors with family, the sumptuous foods, the crunch of snow underfoot as you chased your cousins around the frosted garden, the sharp air rushing into your lungs, the jolly Santa with a real sleigh - this was the spirit of Christmas to me.

So, Christmas in three countries, but only one true feeling of joy.

THOUGH TIME
Lillia Williams

I pity not myself!
For what have I to reap but my own casting.
I sorrow only for those whom I love, and have cut by my own reck-
lessness!
I long not for your touch or the quenching of the passion in my
bones.
I seek only to reconcile our friendship and temper the anguish of
your spirit.
I often recall your beauty!
Your rose red lips as warm as the sun itself, the intoxicating fra-
grance of your smooth flowing body.
I regret that no longer are you mine.
Each night my heart relives what was
Recalling moments of our joy, the times of peace, the instances of
ecstasy.
I remember too the grief, the pain the tears we shared,
But peace or pain with you it was my life and I was content,
You gave me peace,
A serenity of spirit I had never before known,
From a restless river you changed me to a sleepy calm sea.
Only by your understanding and love could it have been fulfilled.
Wisdom you showed me, when inexperience itself ruled my heart,
For your love my spirit calmed.
As the smiling sun calls the wild rose to bloom.
My soul is heavy for your beauty, your heart, your love, like gold
and precious gems
Are worth far more than all I have to give.
Yet throughout the seasons of our lives
I'll always love you!

THE WRITER'S AIDE
Meg McLaren

'No man was more foolish when he had not a pen in his hand, or more wise when he had.' Samuel Johnson

I remember my 15th birthday. My father, arms outstretched, a small oblong package held tenderly, wrapped and tied with silver ribbon. I tore carefully at the tissue paper, revealing a black box, a single word 'Parker' inscribed in bold letters across the top. I gently lifted the lid and there, encased in white satin, lay a Parker 51 Fountain Pen. It was deep red with gold embellishments, my name engraved along the side of the barrel. I unscrewed the top and exposed its hooded, gold nib, iridium tipped and ready to make its first mark.

Man's love affair with writing goes back to our earliest beginnings. Our prehistoric ancestors used sharpened stone and a cave wall to depict significant events in their life stories: hunting, the planting of crops, warlike encounters with other tribes. The first history books.

Communication through the written word, as we know it today, evolved over many hundreds of years. In Greece around 400BC, students of Socrates and Plato might be seen hurrying between marble colonnades and the ornate, gold covered buildings of the Acropolis, carrying scrolls of papyrus or parchment. The words of the philosophers written down using a reed pen fashioned from the hollow, tubular stems of marsh grasses. Busy scribes advised of meetings of the Council, developments in the conflict with Sparta, religious and athletic festivals. Prose and poetry and strange, fantastic tales were recorded for posterity. Using this primitive form of fountain pen, Roman scholars reported new conquests and stories of distant lands. Uprisings and records of taxation were all conveyed in bold strokes using this revolutionary writing instrument.

Then came the Quill Pen, fashioned from the feathers of large birds. This implement dominated our literary achievements for over one thousand years and helped change the course of history. The Magna Carta, the Declaration of Independence and the Constitution of the United States of America were all written using a Quill Pen.

Shakespeare, looking out over the River Avon, would have dipped his Quill and recorded his works that speak to us through time.

The 1880s marked the beginning of a new era; the fountain pen, as we know it today, came on the market. Lewis Waterman led the way, selling his hand-made pens out of the back of a cigar shop. Orders began rolling in and new companies - Parker, Sheaffer and Wahl-Eversharp – were established to fill a growing need.

'Who would have thought that the creativity and inventiveness of man would turn feathers into fountain pens?' Mary Bellis *commented when writing an article about the history of Fountain Pens.*

My Parker 51 was introduced in 1941 and was advertised as "The World's Most Wanted Pen." I am told it is now a collector's item. It was made to be loved and, not unlike a good Claret, has improved over time. It's a sentimental tool, evoking memories of a more relaxed lifestyle, when timeless elegance was possible in everyday occasions and possessions came with a lifetime guarantee.

Fountain pens are not disposable; they are personal, growing with you and changing over time to suit your writing style. Unlike a typewriter or keyboard, a fountain pen reflects our moods in the actual form of the writing, as well as through the words. When I am happy, my letters are rounded and full, when rushed or angry, they trail untidily across the page. I can look back over my journals and know immediately how I was feeling on a particular day, without having to read a single word.

I now own two fountain pens, my original Parker 51 and a Sheaffer. I write in my journal every day, using one of them, and inevitably I recall a classroom in the nineteen fifties: a ceiling fan rocking and spinning overhead, a wooden desk with a white porcelain inkwell filled carefully from a large bottle of 'Quink', into which I dipped my Parker, squeezed and watched the dark line creep to the top of the cartridge. This was a routine that could not be rushed, a time to pause and gather thoughts before committing them to paper. There was little room for mistakes, they could not be disguised and spoilt the finished manuscript.

Mr Phelps, who had been taken prisoner during the Second World War and lived to tell the tale, would walk up and down between the desks, tossing a piece of chalk from hand to hand. Perhaps because of his incarceration and forced seclusion, he loved beautiful things. His own fountain pen, which on occasion he proudly displayed, was a work of art, dark green in colour and inlaid with lacquer. Before setting us a task, he meticulously checked that the ritual had been followed and we were holding our precious implements in the correct manner, not too tightly, not too far down the barrel. When he had satisfied himself that all was in order, he would rap on the nearest desk and my thoughts raced to blackened fingertips, through the curved nib and onto white paper.

We have moved into the age of technology and, in terms of efficiency, nothing can beat my laptop. Sitting at my desk I type, knowing that words, indeed whole sentences and paragraphs, can be deleted or changed by simply pressing a square key. Innumerable ball points and biros are within easy reach around the house. These will do for routine tasks, jotting down lists and the like but nothing can take the place of a fountain pen and the self-esteem that comes from seeing a page of stylish handwriting. Although some call it progress, and I'm sure it is, I wonder sometimes if we haven't lost a lot in the process.

BUTTERFLY TO TIGRESS
Dawn Meredith

In the firelight their dark, beautiful skin shines with grease. Their slim figures are adorned with colourful cloth, the beads clicking together as they move. Celia, in her neat, pale shift dress and sensible sandals, is a dowdy tourist - a plain moth among dazzling butterflies, hovering at the edge of the fire. An elderly woman, Peo Eka, stands regally dressed in a midnight blue robe, her feet bare in the dust. Peo, Celia has found out, means tribal elder, revered woman. Eka is her given name. But why has this woman chosen a tourist perusing clothing racks at the markets to witness this sacred female ceremony? With her gnarled hands Peo Eka raises the largest of three black ceramic bowls and murmurs words in her own tongue. The women echo them respectfully. Then she carefully pours the contents into the middle sized bowl. Black water flows as bits of leaf and small dark berries tumble and plop like unfinished spells. She holds the bowl high.

"Transformation!" she declares, "Butterfly to tigress!" In the flickering, rosy light the dark skinned women release their clothing and dance naked. Drums beat, clapping sticks keep time. Celia stands awkwardly to one side, the smoke making her nostrils and eyes sting.

Peo Eka solemnly spits into the middle sized bowl and passes it around to the other women who pause from their dancing to spit and then pass it on. The pace begins to quicken. Celia can sense the anticipation among the women. With arms raised and eyes closed they sway and grind energetically. Peo Eka pours the black liquid into the final, smallest bowl and beckons Celia to come and stand before her.

Oh my God, what should I do? Every single woman has spat into that concoction! But Celia finds her feet moving forward until she is standing before the elder. Peo Eka stares deep into Celia's eyes.

"I sense pain and longing in you," Peo Eka says in a voice of quiet authority, as if she has witnessed the catastrophe of the last sixteen years of Celia's life. Tears suddenly spring to Celia's eyes. She swallows back down the memories, all the times she almost handed

Charity over to the authorities, unable to cope with a squalling child. Being a mother at fifteen had not been part of her plan. This holiday alone had been a last minute impulse, something she ordinarily would not do.

"Drink!" Urges Peo Eka, shoving the bowl in Celia's face. Celia steps back, her hands raised, feeling panic rise in her chest.

"No. It's fine. Thank you. I'll just watch," she says politely. Peo Eka frowns.

"Butterfly to tigress!" She barks in Delia's face. "Transition! Transformation!" The drums and chanting grow louder. Celia feels the drumbeat throbbing inside her chest. The dance has become erratic, the dancers' eyes wild, their glistening bodies jerking. Sweat begins to trickle down the side of Celia's face.

"Drink!" The elder woman suddenly grabs Celia's hair, tilts back her head and pours the bitter liquid down her throat. The drumbeat stops abruptly and the women cheer. Celia chokes, trying to free herself and stagger away, but the old woman's grip is strong. The liquid spills all over her chin and down her dress. It's too late. She is already contaminated. The leaves and berries stick in her throat. She swallows painfully, trying not to gag. Smells suddenly become overwhelming. The fire is white hot, like a beacon of light burning through her eyes. Distorted, powerful thoughts collide inside Celia's brain. She sways unsteadily on her feet as strong hands grip her arms and lead her to a tatty awning under the trees.

Celia wakes in her hotel bed, dressed in a midnight blue robe reeking of sweat and smoke. She vaguely recalls the events of the night before - Peo Eka, the drums, naked women dancing.

She showers, dresses and sprays perfume to rid herself of the primitive smells still clinging to her body. Hastily she packs her belongings. Her flight isn't until 2 pm but she feels compelled to leave. Closing the door Celia catches a last glimpse of the dirty blue robe lying discarded on the floor.

She arrives at the airport to find her seat has been double booked. Celia loudly demands another seat. Dowdy, quiet Celia never makes demands. On the flight the food is terrible. She complains and is upgraded to a spare seat in first class. The steward can't seem to do enough for her. Puzzled at her own behaviour, Celia tries to sleep.

As she emerges bleary eyed into a Sydney airport lounge Celia scans the group waiting there. Her eyes lock with her daughter's. Charity, bubbly and chatty, takes her heavy bags. With a grateful sigh Celia closes the door on her experience and settles into the passenger seat of her own car.

"How's your driving going?" She asks.

Charity grins. "You've only been gone a week."

At home Charity unpacks Celia's suitcase with curiosity, spreading things on the bed.

"Anything for me?" She asks hopefully.

"A couple of dresses," Celia says tiredly, sitting on a chair in the corner.

"What are these?" Charity holds up two black clay bowls. A third larger bowl lies nestled among Celia's clothes.

Celia's gut drops.

"How did they get there?" Her heart begins beating rapidly. The smells and the visions all come flooding back.

"I love them!" Charity says enthusiastically. "I'm going to try one out." She heads for the bathroom.

"No!" Celia springs to her feet, reaching out. But Charity has already filled the small bowl and drunk from it. Celia snatches it from her.

"Don't touch my things!" She hisses, feeling heat crawl into her face. Charity stares at her, mouth open.

"Mum… What's the matter? It's only a silly bowl."

"Do not touch my things," Celia repeats in a low voice.

"Why? We share everything anyway. What's the big deal?" Celia looks at the child she bore sixteen years ago, the child she has always been too weak to discipline properly.

"Not anymore," she says firmly. Peo Eka's words echo inside her brain - *Butterfly to tigress.* Charity's eyes narrow.

"You can't tell me what to do," she relies haughtily, her pert nose in the air.

"I am your mother," Celia replies confidently, staring her down.

"So what?" Scowling, Charity snatches up the small bowl, a malicious glint in her eye.

"Put it down, Charity."

"Fine" the girl says, with a defiant look, then hurls the clay bowl at the wall. But to Charity's dismay the bowl bounces and lands in Celia's outstretched hands. Celia looks at her shocked daughter calmly.

"From now on, you will do as I ask. Understood?"

"Mum, what's happened?" Charity's voice is a squeak. "You're scaring me."

"No. I'm waking up." Celia walks to the window, bowl cradled in her hands. A bright, sunny day presents itself. And so does an idea. Celia slides back the wardrobe doors revealing her huge collection of colourful, sparkly, amazing shoes. Looking down at her feet, deformed since birth, she smiles to herself. Fetching a large garbage bag she fills it with all the beautiful shoes she has never worn.

"Mum, what are you doing?" Charity shrieks.

"Transforming," replies Celia grimly, shoving the glittering things into the bag until the wardrobe is empty.

"But you love them!" Charity pleads. "Please, Mum. Don't throw them away. I wear them sometimes, you know!"

Celia glances up, looking at her daughter as if for the first time. The girl's thick makeup is like a mask.

"Not anymore," Celia replies. Satisfied with her task she straightens and smiles, opening her arms wide. Charity hesitates, her face bathed in the sunlight streaming through the bedroom window. She looks twelve again. Kind of lost.

"Mum, what happened to you?" She whispers, standing there.

"Butterfly to tigress," replies Celia. "Come on, give your mum a hug." As her arms clasp around her daughter Celia breathes in the scent of the girl's clean washed hair and feels the weight of a very heavy burden fall away, like smoke drifting from the embers of a fire, up, up into the cool, starry night.

SCHOOLS OF THOUGHT
Graeme Hetherington

Locked out of classrooms we ate our
Cribs brought from home in 'shelter sheds',
Though they were open to the West

Coast's almost daily wind and rain.
One for each sex and built apart
At opposite ends of the yard,

The Head made lightning raids but failed
To keep us separate. I learnt
Not to expect too much, since far

From ideal, my 'better half's' talk
Demeaned no less than that of boys,
Pasties tasting as a fart smells,

Menstrual rags of rotten fish.
Then sent to a male boarding school
At thirteen I was able to

Indulge my horror of the flesh,
Become a Dante mooning for,
No real Beatrice glimpsed as soul mate,

But a mentally perilous,
Totally insubstantial dream,
A hope that an as yet unknown

Form of perfection would appear,
Recognised as such when it did.
Disastrously, it never has,

My marriages, affairs, wrecked by
The shadow of pure abstract thought
That at most she was second best.

MYSTERY
Jacqueline Lonsdale Cuerton

"Good morning, ladies. What are we going to do today?"

"How about we go over to the Community Hall and discuss it over coffee?"

"That's okay by me; what about you, Jacki?"

Marion and Ruth turned to the third woman, "Yes, that's fine as long as it isn't crowded."

"Oh, it's too early to be crowded," said Ruth, "in fact we're earlier than usual, aren't we? You usually have morning coffee with Bruce, anyway. What happened this morning, aren't you speaking or something?"

"Don't be ridiculous, Ruth, we're not tied at the hip, you know. He's having a lie-in."

Marion and Ruth exchanged quick glances and Marion, the smoother of ruffled feathers, said, "that's nice; let's go then. If it is quiet, we can have a game of Scrabble."

"Uh, oh, Brigitte's there – now it is early for her. She'll want to join us and Jacki, you know you can't help fighting with her."

"No I don't. She fights with me."

"Come on, don't let us start. There's three of us, one of her, we'll manage." Marion threaded an arm through one of her two companions and headed for the doorway.

Ruth chuckled, "Just look at her; do you think she's trying for a job as a store-window mannequin?"

Marion, more seriously, her arms now free, mused she looked exactly like that when she left the club house last night with her husband. Jacki said again, "leave her alone, she was always making eyes at my Bruce. Hateful woman."

"She doesn't look natural," Marion said as she started towards her. Jacki grabbed her arm, "Leave her alone, she's a bitch", she spat.

"No", said Ruth, "she hasn't stirred, not a muscle. You'd think our noise would wake her, or something."

"Oh, leave her alone", shouted Jacki again.

Ruth caught Marion's arm, "Don't touch her, Marion. I think we should ring Deidre, get her here. She is the Manager, after all."

"Yes, you're right. I've got her number in my phone."

"Me too", and Ruth was already dialling.

The looks between these two women said they were thinking the same thing but neither wanted to say it out loud. They would leave that pronouncement to someone else.

Twenty minutes later the place was buzzing with police, detectives, the forensic pathologist. The doors to the community centre had been closed and a couple of constables outside were trying to keep the growing crowd of residents living in this retirement village away from the windows. Marion and Ruth were inside, together, Deidre was a little distance to one side. Marion didn't notice her husband being ushered in a little while later.

"So when you two ladies came in, was anyone else here, apart from the deceased?" asked the Chief Inspector.

The two women gave a little start, looking around, "No", said Ruth,"there were three of us; where's Jacki?"

"So who is this Jacki?"

Ruth replied, "well, she lives here, too. We meet, usually meet on a Wednesday morning, have a coffee and spend a couple of hours or so with her".

"Do you meet with her on other days?"

"Not by arrangement", offered Marion. "If I, and Ruth too, I would think, bump into her, it's a quick hello and carry on with whatever we intended doing."

"When did you last see her?"

Ruth picked up again, "She was walking down from her place and joined Marion and me. We continued on to here, for a coffee and we thought we might play Scrabble or something. I saw Brigitte through the window" – Marion made a suppressed snort at that point and people turned to her.

"Sorry," she said, "Ruth made a joke about her being a store-window model. It was funny. Sorry."

"What happened then, Mrs Bentham." The Chief Inspector turned back to Ruth.

"Well, Jacki sort of went slightly hysterical. We were inside then and Marion was going towards Brigitte because she didn't look, well, she didn't look quite right. Jacki really yelled to leave her alone. We, Marion and I, were sort of concentrated on Brigitte and rang Deidre, Mrs Joffrey, the manager here. And then you came."

While this was happening one of the police officers had asked the manager for the house number of Jacki and sent a couple, male and female officers, to bring her, and her husband, here.

The Chief asked for this to be done, was told it was underway already when the two officers returned minus the couple. "All locked up, car gone. Neighbour said she'd seen the woman fly in. She said she and her husband threw a few things in the car and sped off. Above the speed limit we have here, she sniffed, could have killed someone."

"So tell me ladies, who were the deceased's friends? Who did she spend time with?"

Marion and Ruth looked at each other. "Well, I don't know", ventured Marion. "I can't think of anyone she was consistently with. Can you Ruth?"

"Come to think of it, no. The only place I'd see her would be in here and she'd be with a group playing cards or some other game."

"And the missing Jacki, what about her friends?"

"Mmm", started Ruth, "bit the same really. Of course she had her husband, 'her Bruce', but apart from Marion and me on a Wednesday morning, that was about it. And we're not really friends, these Wednesdays just sort of happened."

"Do you think she was not popular?"

"Oh, that's a hard one. Not fair either, really", said Marion.

Ruth offered, "she was a bit of a busy-body and did, you know, flirt, with all the men."

"Including yours?" The chief addressed both women.

"Well, mine. Ruth is a widow; spared the circus."

"And how do you react to that, Mrs Smith?"

"Oh, we just take it in our stride, I suppose. My husband can be quite rude to her, and I've told him off about that but Brigitte never seemed to be affected by it."

Ruth giggled but when all eyes swung in her direction, she became sober again. "Sorry", she said, "but it was funny most times. Neil, Marion's husband, can be quite biting, clever in the way he can say things, so for someone who wanted to think she was being paid a compliment, that's what it was. Everyone else was in on the joke. I don't know why she thought everyone was after her husband; if I were her I'd be pleased if someone took him off my hands."

"Ruth", Marion admonished.

"Yes, sorry."

At this point the Chief asked where Jacki and her husband were, was told they had left the village, seemingly in a hurry.

"So you're not considered a threat Mrs Bentham?" asked a female officer.

"Oh no, I'm not pretty enough, for one thing".

"By whose standards?" Ruth was asked as the officer appraised Ruth's clear skin, even features.

"Oh, Jacki told me that, not 'her Bruce's' type at all. Jacki is quite vain, forever comparing herself with others."

"What about you, Mrs Smith? Are you not pretty enough either?"

"Don't know if I'm pretty enough, she chuckled, but 'her Bruce' doesn't like the intellectual type either and apparently that's what I am." Marion had painted the quotation marks in the air with her fingers around 'intellectual'

"Don't know why we're friends with her at all, really," muttered Ruth.

"What about the deceased – did she have friends?"

"There are very few meaningful friendships in this place", volunteered Marion. "You buy a house here, think, surely with 450 or so homes here there must be a resident or two one can be friends with. And who knows, that might deepen over time. I was lucky Ruth was here. But really, most of the women here behave like silly schoolgirls who haven't grown out of those schoolgirl crushes. Jacki, most of them, I think, is insecure so jealousies soon flare up. I was lucky meeting Neil so many years ago. Lucky life, eh?"

Brigitte's next–of–kin had to be traced and notified. Marion's husband had been questioned and agreed with what his wife had said about seeing Brigitte on the lounge by the window. Those in the room were cautioned about not speaking to anyone, anyone at all, about the situation.

A few days later a constable said to his sergeant, "Hey Sarge, I've found a sister for that dead woman at the home."

"Where is she?"

"You'll never guess ..."

"Which is why we're not in the guessing game, the officer snapped. Where is she, Constable?"

"At that very same place, what'ya call it? Diamondtina Village."

"What? The same place? Why the hell hasn't she come forward? Come on. Let's go visit."

A woman, badly disfigured by burns answered the door."

"Mrs Cracknell, Amelia Cracknell?"

"Yes, you'd better come in. I've been wondering how long it would take you."

The two police officers were introduced to Mrs Cracknell's husband, Royce. "Yes", she added, "even looking like this I met a man who could love me."

"Mrs Cracknell, was your sister aware of your residing here?"

"No. No one knew, just us." Darling, she turned to her husband, "can you get that photo ...? Yes," she said, "that's what I looked like previously. No comparison."

"Perhaps you could tell us your story, Mrs Cracknell."

"Well, I was engaged, not to Royce, someone else. My fiancée had come to stay for a few days; his job took him away from town for several weeks at a time. It was separate bedrooms then, my parents would have been ... shocked, ashamed, if we'd slept together before marriage. At least they were spared finding out what did go on under their roof. I didn't know at the time. My fiancée got along well with them and my sister and I was glad about that. I thought we were going to be a happy, united family.

"The house caught fire. About eleven in the evening. Summer. You probably read about it. It was a funny house, the ways the rooms were arranged. My parents and I had our rooms on one side, my sister's and the spare were on the other. I found out later, the fire was fiercest on my side. They said it was due to an electrical fault. Neighbours said they saw my fiancée throwing paintings out of the front door. Someone they couldn't name was stacking them in a small truck. He'd gone by the time anyone mentioned him. I didn't ever see them, the paintings I mean, again.

"It seems I had tried to get out but I was overcome by fire and smoke. My parents died in their bed. My fiancée rescued my sister – pretty easy really as they were in the same room. He came to see me, once, in hospital, said he'd always loved my sister and was marrying her. I don't know how it happened but my sister and he got all the insurance. I was too ill to bother with any business and then I just didn't care. I'd lost everything I'd ever loved, I didn't want to live. I met Royce in Rehab. I couldn't understand how he could be so nice, gentle, kind – I looked worse then than I do now." She looked up at him, perched on the arm of the settee where she sat. He disengaged his hand from hers to stretch his arm across her back and squeezed her closer.

"My visits to Rehab lessened but Royce found excuses to call in to where I was staying. He asked me out for dinner when he judged me strong enough to go out in public. I couldn't understand how he could be seen with this monster." He leaned over and kissed the top of her head.

Amelia continued. "Royce helped me to not see myself as a monster but as the person I'd always been. But I could never be that, I had hate in my heart now, for those two people. They did well, no doubt using whatever he got for the paintings and the insurance. I was in a weakened state and their solicitors were very good at getting me to sign various bits of paper. But we've been alright, haven't we Darling. Royce works part-time now, looks after me all the time. We have a beautiful son who has a lovely wife and two gorgeous children. We go to grandparents' day at their school and do everything else grandparents do."

"The kids love her", Royce put in. "The two classes ask questions about the scars in that honest, refreshing way children have."

"Yes", interrupted Amelia, "they are learning about acceptance."

"And even with her almost webbed fingers, Amelia can make the most wonderful craft pieces."

She took a sip of the tea made earlier by Royce; "I'll finish the story", she said.

"My sister's husband left her after a few years. Everything was in his name. She fought for what she considered hers but as she'd never stopped working and should have been independently wealthy, she got very little. She was never a saver, though, so not much in the bank. She wrote to me then, via my solicitor, asking for help. I asked my solicitor to reply, saying I was not in any position to do anything for her. She ended up here, in one of the rentals and government assistance. And then, blow-me-down, the ex-husband married Jacki. She was already living here. Bought with her first husband who died quite young. They look as if they've been together forever. He wouldn't know I or Brigitte was here. B. would have had her friends, Jacki hers and we have ours – and never the twain shall meet. Except for Marion and Ruth. They are our friends but because Marion is particularly kind she and Ruth took pity on Jacki who seemed so lonely, even with 'her Bruce', and so had this loose arrangement on Wednesdays. They don't know anything about relationships, the family connections."

So who killed Brigitte? Murdered, poisoned by the juice of some exotic leaves growing here.

Analysis showed a rarely-used poison, traced back to a plant growing in a small part of the Highlands of New Guinea. Further questioning elicited Amelia and Brigitte had spent their early growing years in PNG. Jacki and 'her Bruce' were still missing. Amelia was questioned at length. Detectives re-examined the home and garage of Jacki and Bruce. Bank statements showed regular payments into what was found to be Brigitte's account. The garage showed Bruce to be a wine-maker. Further examination found traces of the plant on the equipment. They were now hunting a killer.

Once caught, it didn't take long for Bruce to cave-in. Yes, he'd recently made wine; yes, he'd ground up the leaves to make the poison and added it to one bottle, the bottle that arrived at Brigitte's door with the note, 'From an Admirer'.

Ah ha, thought Brigitte, when she found it, I'll have to find this 'admirer' but first let's see if he can make decent wine. It was a light, pleasant drink, leaving a slight bitterness in the mouth. The empty bottle was still in the kitchen.

By-and-by the whole story came out. Bruce had claimed on the insurance, a signature of Brigitte's and a forged one of Amelia's doctor who allegedly had stated his patient agreed with the arrangements. Amelia was, after all, officially still Bruce's fiancée. The money went into his bank account.

Brigitte's blackmailing began when she found out her ex-husband was here with Jacki.

Bruce was found guilty of murder and Jacki guilty of being an accessory before the fact. Once jailed, further evidence brought the charge of arson against Bruce. That is still on-going.

He is likely to be in jail for a very long time.

MAD AS MAD
Kim Peart

Dad went mad
found naked on the wood
holding an axe
wasn't good

All the chooks were beheaded
one still running around
nowhere fast
the cat was never found

The dogs had been hit by a car
both dead
waiting to be buried
"Would you like to be fed?"

Aunt Matilda thought that'd work
get the bugger down
but Dad was busy swearing
news had reached town

A siren could be heard
there may be no happy ending
the neighbours dog was barking
people were staring

Then Dad snapped out of it
went in for tea with gran
never happened again
just mad as mad

FORGOTTEN TREASURE
Dawn Meredith

Chapter One

'I never thought you'd be so excited about a second hand sofa,' said Mum, jostling nanobites on the frypan.

'It's purple and I love it!' shouted Robina and did a cartwheel in the kitchen, crashing into the bin. 'Oops. Sorry.' She adjusted her proximity sensor. 'Mum, I'm hungry. Can I have some polymer prunes?'

'Dinner's almost ready. We're having baked techtoids and dumplings tonight.'

'Yum! What's for dessert?'

'Your favourite - cupcakes.' Mum smiled.

'Yay! Can I eat dinner on the new sofa?'

'Do you want it to look and smell like the old one, then?' asked Dad, laying the placemats on the carousel. Robina frowned. Their old sofa smelled like wet dog and mouldy food. It was because she had trouble with her ladle gripper sometimes, spilling food and drink.

'No,' she admitted, wrinkling her smell sensor. 'This one's special. When I grow up I'm going to keep it in my own house!'

'Are you?' Chuckled Dad. He pressed the drop delivery button. It dropped cups and plates exactly in the middle of each placemat as the carousel turned. CLICK, CLICK, CLICK. Dad plopped blue nanoberry juice into the cups. Mum dished up and they all sat down to eat.

After dinner Robina rushed into the lounge room to cuddle up to the new sofa. She buried herself under the cushions and made a cubby house with a blanket. Then she took off all the cushions to investigate underneath. The fabric was black with white spots, like a giant lady bug. And springy. She bounced once, twice, three times....

'Ouch!' Something sharp pierced her footpad. She reached down and probed carefully. Down there, behind the padded back, an object was stuck. Robina clicked on a rubber endpiece and thrust down, pushing past the sharp staples that held the fabric tight. Her vision sensor turned on the infra-red beam. Sticking her tongue out to concentrate better, she gently pulled. The object was slowly coming loose. At last she held it up - a bag of thick, tough material, smelling musty and damp, like Dad's tool shed. Robina undid the stiff flap at the top. She was about to put her hand inside when she heard footsteps.

'Robina, what on earth...' Dad stood in the doorway, frowning, his arms folded over his big chest.

Chapter Two
'I found something Dad!' Robina held up the bulging bag. 'Treasure!' Dad took it gently from her. He looked inside. Then he drew out bitcredit – hundreds and hundreds of pieces.

'We're rich!' shouted Robina, jumping up and down on the sofa. 'Woo hoo!'

'Hang on a second,' said Dad. 'This bitcredit isn't ours.'

'But I found it!' Robina protested. Dad was shaking his head.

'We will have to find the previous owners of the sofa.'

'But how will we do that, Dad? We bought it from a second-hand assembly line outlet.'

'We'll find them, don't worry,' Dad said firmly. Robina scowled.

'But Dad, think of all the things we could buy with that bitcredit! A new home gantry for you even!'

'No, Robina,' Dad said, and the look on his face made her go quiet. 'That bitcredit does not belong to us. We must do everything we can to return it.'

Robina was unhappy. Why should she give it back? The owner had probably forgotten by now. Sitting on her bed she thought about all the fabulous things she could do with the bitcredit. And became angry at Dad for spoiling it all.

Chapter Three
Robina was still unhappy the next day when Dad dropped her off at school. He was on his way to the second hand assembly line outlet. Robina told her best friend Maisie all about it. Maisie agreed that only a very stupid person would leave bitcredit down the back of a sofa and they probably didn't miss it.

After school, Robina was not in a hurry to get home. She slinked through the front door, past the lounge room and into her bedroom. She didn't even want to sit on the purple sofa anymore. Mum came in to talk to her.

'Robina, are you still upset about the bitcredit you found?' Robina didn't answer. She picked up a teddy and scowled at its happy face. 'I understand it's an exciting discovery,' continued Mum. 'But what if the owner has been looking everywhere for it? What if they need it badly?'

'Then they should have put it in the bank, instead of the sofa!' Robina said crossly. She dropped the teddy and crossed her arms.

'Giving the bitcredit back is the right thing to do,' Mum said softly and left the room.

Soon, Dad's car pulled up in the driveway. Robina heard the front portal squeak open. She crept out of her room and down the hall to hide behind the kitchen entry and listen to her parents talking.

'I didn't tell them how much we'd found,' Dad was saying. 'They said they'd pass on the message.' He sighed. 'It's a lot of bitcredit. Twenty thousand pieces. Somewhere, someone is terribly worried about it.'

Robina clapped a handcup over her taste sensor to stop a scream of excitement escaping. *Twenty thousand pieces?*

Chapter Four

That evening the shrill alarm of the external connection rang. From her bed, Robina heard Dad speaking quietly. Then he said, 'No, no, really! That's not necessary.' Then he said goodbye and hung up. Robina padded down the hall.

'Dad, who was that? Was it the owner?'

'Robina, what are you doing out of bed?'

'Please Dad, just tell me, do we have to give the bitcredit back?'

Dad frowned. 'Are you still thinking we can keep it? I thought we'd taught you better than that.' Robina hung her head and slinked off back to her room. It took ages to switch off into downtime. She kept thinking of all the sparkling, thrilling, amazing things she could do with twenty thousand pieces.

In the morning Mum announced that they would all be going to visit the previous owner of the sofa. Robina was even going to miss an hour of school.

'Why do I have to go?' Robina complained. But Mum and

Dad just looked at each other and smiled.

The car pulled up at a nice wooden dwelling with a wide, green lawn. A lady unit and two small copy-canines came running out to meet them. Robina giggled when one of them licked her hand-cup. The lady unit said her name was Magnetia. When Dad offered her the canvas bag of bitcredit she just smiled and said, 'You keep hold of it for now.' They all trooped inside the house and were offered nanojuice and hollow helix crackers. Then an elderly lady unit shuffled in. Her cyclo drive was worn out and she listed to one side.

'And you must be Robina,' she said kindly, extending her end-effector. Robina shook it gently. Looking up into the lady unit's faded blue visual sensors Robina couldn't help smiling at her.

'This is my mother, Hildix,' said Magnetia. 'She has just moved into a retirement village. There wasn't room for her favourite sofa, so we had to sell it,' she explained. Hildix sat down and smiled at Robina.

'You like my sofa?'

Robina grinned. 'It's smells much nicer than our old one.'

Magnetia continued. 'Anyway, as I told your Dad last night, Robina, I sold the sofa but I had no idea my mother had stored all her savings inside it. So when I told her it was gone...'

Robina gasped. 'Your savings?' she whispered, staring at the elderly unit.

'Yes,' said Hildix, nodding soberly. 'For the last thirty cycles I've been putting aside a little bit each week.'

Robina gulped. How could she take this old lady's bitcredit? Tears welled up inside her visual sensor sockets. 'I'm so sorry!' she blurted. 'I wasn't going to keep it, really I wasn't!'

'I know,' said Hildix. 'There are honest citizens in the world after all.' She smiled at Robina's parents. Dad got to his feet and handed the canvas bag, not to Hildix, but to Robina.

'Robina, give this back to its rightful owner?'

'Here you are, Hildix,' Robina said shyly. Hildix thanked her and opened the bag on her lap. Her stiff end-effectors struggled with the flap. 'It's all there, I promise!' Robina assured her. Hildix nodded, but kept counting out bitcredit pieces. Robina just stood there awkwardly, not knowing what to do. Finally Hildix looked up.

'Robina, you are such a lovely young unit, so honest. It makes an old entity like me very happy. I want you to have this.' She picked up one of Robina's handcups and folded something into it. Robina opened her handcup and stared. Bitcredit. Lots of it.

'But…' she tried to say.

'It's a reward. For giving my savings back to me. One thousand bitcredits.' Hildix grinned at Robina's shocked face. She tickled Robina under the chin. 'Spend it wisely my little friend!'

Robina kissed Hildix's cheek and thanked her. Her primary pump felt all buzzy with excitement. She was already dreaming about a nice present she was going to buy, for a lady unit who had just moved into a retirement village.

THE BURU SHADOW
Jennie Herrera

Should you travel where the Buru shadow falls?
Should you spend where soccer stadiums run red?
Should you stay where car windows are tinted black
and bodyguards stand burly and impenetrable?

Should you visit where it's well documented that
the secret police have been extra hard at work?
Should you book your holiday and make certain your
room is soundproof against a mother's screams?

Should you read up well on the trail of torture sales,
before you turn to those lovely glossy brochures?
Should you take out a sub to Amnesty before you decide?
Should you only go where people's lives are respected

and where there's no fighting going on, inside or outside
a country's border—and where they never sell arms
to fuel wars in faraway places where the pain can be
overlooked—and where the crying of children without legs

need not be heard in the boardroom or the factory floor?
What standards should you set yourself? Where should you go
that your snaps will never need apologizing for? Is there
anywhere? Or should you stay at home—and feel a sense

of vague disquiet—that home hardly passes your stringent test—
and then you wonder if the only thing left to do if you're going
to live with your conscience, that shadow there, is take your
vacation money and send it off somewhere and tell your friends

next time they ask: there's nowhere, I'm afraid, (you say sadly)
unless I choose a desert island, an offshore rock, a place unpopulated,
a boat, a raft, something from which I need never land again;
a way to escape the shadow, the regret, the guilt, and take my holiday
in a tiny patch of perfect sun …

OVERHEARD IN A PUB
Allan Jamieson

"What's the book about?"

"It's about the Bible; well worth reading."

"*Geez* – I didn't know you were bent that way, Baz!"

"Don't worry, I'm not. I'm well past the biblical three score years and ten, yet I've never *tried* to read the Good Book. Instead, I've just finished reading this book written by a bloke who *did* read it." [*God – a Biography*, by Jack Miles © 1996, Knopf first edition]

"So, still pretty dry for a topic, isn't it?"

"Not at all! Miles taught himself Hebrew so he could read the several versions of the Bible written in that language."

"So, there's more than one Good Book is there?"

"At least two, but this 'biography' is really fascinating. Anyway, it was when Miles dealt with Wisdom that I sat up; *this* was absolutely astonishing to my mind. The words of Wisdom (in Proverbs, the 28th Book of the Hebrew Bible, the *Tanakh*) are those of a woman. For instance:

'Wisdom cries out in the streets,
Raises her voice in the squares.
…
You dullards hate knowledge;
You are indifferent to my rebuke;
I will now speak my mind to you,
…
When terror comes like a disaster,
…
When trouble and distress comes upon you,
Then they shall call me but I will not answer;
…
Because they hated knowledge,
And did not choose fear of the Lord;
…
But he who listens to me will dwell in safety,
Untroubled by the terror of misfortune.'"   [Proverbs 1:20-33. As
                                                                per Miles p. 293-4]

"So, God made her just like he made us, did he?"

"Must you always begin with 'So'?"

"Sorry Baz."

"No, He did not. According to Wisdom:

'The Lord created me as the beginning of His course
As the first of His works of old.
In the distant past I was fashioned,
At the beginning, at the origin of earth.
…
He had not yet made earth and fields,
Or the world's first clumps of clay.
I was there when He set the heavens into place;
…
I was with Him as a confidant,
A source of delight every day,
…
For he who finds me finds life
And obtains favour from the Lord.
But he who misses me destroys himself;
All who hate me love death.'"   [Proverbs 8:22-9:6. As per Miles p.295]

"Wow! God was no fool, eh Baz. I always wondered about Him. The impression is that He sat up there alone in the clouds and created the World in seven days. Of course, nobody believes the seven days then were like seven days now. I'll bet He spent many of those days away from that task while He found 'delight' with His first creation. He was just like us, eh! He never let on that He had a floosy at his beck and call!"

"That's true and that is one reason why the Wisdom chapter hit me square between the eyes. I mean, she *is* the smarter one of the two; God's errors and stupidities are described in book after book of the Bible, and *boy* there were a lot of these, but God never acknowledges her. *That's* what floored me: think of world history; a never-ending litany of war, chaos and pestilence through thousands of years, and why? Because MEN have run the world and women have *never* been listened to in all that time. Miles (p. 405) noted that, 'the feminine was not merely absent from the developed character of God, but had been excluded from it … God spoke of himself as the plural and saw himself reflected in the human couple rather than the human male [thereafter] the female in the divine male was suppressed.' Mankind – 'made in His image' – *still* does not acknowledge her."

"Should we think of Wisdom as God's wife? If so, who married them?"

"Miles writes (p. 297), 'we may infer that she is to be considered, at least metaphorically, as God's wife.' The Bible contains only this one description of what a wife is:

'What a rare find is a capable wife!
Her worth is far beyond that of rubies.
Her husband puts his confidence in her,
…
She is good to him, never bad,
…
She looks for wool and flax,
And sets her hand to them with a will.
She is like a merchant fleet,
Bringing her food from afar.
She rises while it is still night,
And supplies provisions for her household,
…
She sets her mind on an estate and acquires it;
…
And performs her tasks with vigor.' [Proverbs 31:10-19.
As per Miles p.296-7]

Those words were not supposed to have been said by God; one of the many contributors to the Bible must have thought them worth putting down for posterity."

"In other words, Baz, no matter what we choose to call them, women are but beasts of burden in Man's eyes."

"Unfortunately, you're right! God saw – and we men see – the female sex in only a limited sense; we still have yet to understand the real core strength of females, their *wisdom*. In Proverbs Wisdom doesn't pull her punches:

'Lazybones, go to the ant;
Study its ways and learn.
Without leaders, officers or rulers,
It lays up its stores during the summer,

Gathers in its food at the harvest.
How long will you lie there, lazybones;
When will you wake from your sleep?
A bit more sleep, a bit more slumber,
A bit more hugging yourself in bed,
And poverty will come calling upon you.' ...   [Proverbs 6:6-11.
                                                 As per Miles p.300]

By contrast, God tells us His power is sufficient for us; we do not need to make any effort of our own. By 'us' it would seem God is talking directly to us men – you and me. That's why MAN has made such a mess of things."

"Yeah, Baz. I'm beginning to see that women have good reason to be pissed off."

"Miles sums up Wisdom (p.302) as follows: 'She remains distinct from [God] by representing, instead, collective humanity'. All of us – men and women – must work together to build a just world."

"It's my shout, Baz – same again?"

==//==//==

"Ah, that is good! My old beer was getting warm."

"So, any other news?"

"There you go with that 'So' again."

"Oh, alright. What else is new?"

"Here's an interesting thing and it relates well to what I was just saying. As you know my wife is Japanese and at lunch today, she told me of a news item from NHK on SBS2. Have you heard of the board game called Go?"

"No. Is it like chess?"

"Far more challenging, because the options are far greater and the rules are way simpler. Go could be envisaged as like a naval battle at sea, while chess is like a battle on land. The task in Go is to surround one or more pieces ('ships') of your opponent and thereby remove ('sink') them. It's a war of attrition."

"Alright, I've got a rough picture. Is Go an ancient game?"

"Go has been around for 5,000 years. The news is that eleven players were admitted to the World Professional Go ranks yesterday, in various divisions, and eight of these were girls – the youngest was only ten years old! I couldn't believe how perfectly this illustrated what Wisdom was on about – we lazybones haven't taken the hint and studied the ant."

"Maybe it's too late now, Baz."

"Yes, I reckon us men are going to be swamped by a *tsunami* of hugely talented women, who will show us how to really run this World. I can't wait to see that – assuming I don't get drowned in the process."

"Let's drink to that."

VERSES WHILE MINDING THE TARKINE SHOP 2005
TARKINE DREAMING
Lesley Podmore - 2005

Pure joy, a flight to heaven's door,
Feet still enmeshed in Earth's own floor;
  Soft earth;
Small creatures, twigs, old leaves "a-rust".

A movement -----
   wombat holes and prints of quolls
Are glimpsed among the bark, the litter;
Small birds scavenge, hop and twitter.

  Drops of dew,
  Drops of rain,
  Pitter patter down again.

Breeze blows;
Breeze blew here -----   before   -----
The Nature Spirits, ancient ones who watch in love,
Here do their work ----
Work of timeless growth and care,
Nurture still -----   creating here.

Who are we to interfere?

NEMESIS
Graeme Hetherington

With pick and knife, I twice attacked
My brother, then I left him, leg
Gashed when the truck we rode derailed
Because I wouldn't use the brake
Despite his begging to get off.

As next he did the swing I pushed
And pushed from hatred of his bliss-
Fed face, that landed flat on blocked
Tear ducts the doctors' many probes
Failed even medically to fix,

Let alone problems of the heart,
My eyes now also watering, but
From age instead of the remorse
I think I ought to feel, yet can't,
When he was loved and I was not.

TUMBLING ON
Lotta M King

Sometimes there is a future,
the time of sweet belonging,
of knowing who you are,

where the counterpane of dreams
has known fields
with paths and directions
marked and unremarkable,

the stupefaction of acceptance
of knowing no change
beside the unfolding days.

Lives are disordered, unseasonal,
abrupt.
We changelings know not who
we will be
as the world turns.

The sunlight sometimes falls
obtusely, upon a wooded hill,
lighting the ground and trunks
in unwitnessed ways.

As the sunlight always falls
so,
life always rises.

THE FINAL RESTING PLACE OF AIDAN MURPHY
Meg McLaren

Bridget comes here once a week
To tidy up and lay fresh flowers.
A quiet place where prayerful angels listen.
She swings open a rusting Iron Gate.
Steps onto a graveled path that twists.

There is comfort here,
Moving in and out of the shadows.
In the mists of memory she sees her baby,
Asleep in a box lined with velvet.
His hands are curled into tight fists.

It was mid-winter when Aidan died.
Frost lay white upon the hard earth,
The eucalypts whispered.
They sent Josh out along Rob's road.
'Find Cormac, and bring him home.'

Sitting by the fire, she held her son in her arms.
She sang to him in Gaelic,
As her mother had to her.
She rubbed his feet and waited for Cormac.
Tears furrowed her face.

'My darling, my love.'
Cormac's voice breaks and he closes his eyes.
Wraps his arms around her.
'He's cold.' Bridget hears herself.
And the little dog, whimpers his distress.

So Bridget comes here once a week.
She lingers beneath an old gum tree.
Finds relief among the headstones,
Listing like a field of corn

Blown in the wind.

She speaks his name to her heart.
She believes he is secure among relatives,
The Lions of Erin,
Gone before, in bloody protest.
Her father with them, playing his melodeon.

Bridget stays until the world calls,
And she must go.

AUTHOR BIOGRAPHIES

GRAEME BOURKE

In 1985 Graeme took up fly fishing in Tasmania and during this journey he kept a diary which was used to produce his first non-fiction book *Come Fly Fish With Me*, which has now been put up as an ebook. This book received wide acclaim from the fly fishing fraternity. He then completed a correspondence course on writing and began writing articles for sporting and travel magazines. In 2008 he published his second book on fishing *If Only The World Would Go Fishing*.

His main ambition was to write fiction, so in 2010 he published *Hawkins' Grove* which has also been converted to an ebook. These three books are available in hard copy from "Window on the World" bookshop in Ulverstone, Tasmania. *Mountain Pride*, *The Ghost Ship*, *The Gates of Hell* and *The House of Dreams* are only available as ebooks.

In June of 2014 Graeme uploaded the first book in his trilogy *The Orphan and the Shadow Walker: The Awakening*. The feedback has been very positive. Sales from the second and third book have been encouraging. *An Ancient Warrior* is his most recent fiction novel.

Graeme writes book reviews for a local newsletter and from these he has compiled the best of these reviews; if you are looking for a book to read he guarantees you will find something here. He has just published a new book called *A Fortunate Destiny*, a love story set in the early seventies. *Tears in Thailand* has now been published as well; this is a true story telling of Graeme's journey in Thailand, his experiences and emotions as he finds happiness in the land of smiles.

For more, see

<https://www.smashwords.com/profile/view/GraemeBourke>

JACQUELINE LONSDALE CUERTON

Jacqueline Lonsdale Cuerton likes to write. English was her best subject but she needed to make a living and becoming a writer was out of the question. It was after she retired that writing took hold and she enjoys 'the writing life'. She has been relatively successful, became a Creative Writing tutor, both in paid and volunteer capacities. She didn't think she was a short story writer but found she had enough to send to her publisher which were accepted for publication (in about October, 2019).

The same publisher, Ginninderra Press, published her life story, *The Last Shot*, last December, but it all started with poetry and *The Eyes Have It*, which was published in 2012. Prior to that, Jacqueline had self-published a novel, *The In-Between Man* and *Around The World in 80 Poems*, a rhyming account of her twelve-months around-the-world travel. She is quick to say, it is not poetry, it just rhymes, an exercise she set herself and enjoyed doing. As the publisher said, it is not everybody's cup of tea. It has some very contrived lines to assist with the rhyming and while she has been told she ought to make it into a travel memoir, she likes it the way it is. She says it makes her laugh.

ANT DRY

ANT DRY moved from Zimbabwe to Tasmania in 2007.   He has lived in the Burnie area since then with his wife, Yvonne. Their four children live on the mainland. He sees himself as the most contented person on the planet, after all, who could ask for more from life than living in Tasmania and having the world's most wonderful family?

JENNIE HERRERA

Jennie Herrera currently lives in Hobart and is President of the Tasmanian FAW. She has had some success with short stories (including winning the Max Harris Short Story Award), poetry (including the Gwen Harwood Poetry Prize) and twice winning the VIC FAW Alan Marshall Award for a novel manuscript for *The Vigil* and *Old Postcards* and the Michele Turner Award for a book manuscript about East Timor with *The Set of the Sun*. Some of her writing is available at https://jlherrera.com

GRAEME HETHERINGTON

[Portrait image courtesy of *Australian Book Review*]

Born in Tasmania's Latrobe in 1937, my first thirteen years were spent on the island's West Coast where I attended the Rosebery and Zeehan state schools before going to boarding school in Launceston for five years and then on to the University of Tasmania. As a teacher in the Classics Department there for over a quarter of a century I fell in love with European culture and have lived much of my life in that part of the world trying to flesh out what I taught which was nowhere to be found in Australia.

In 2013, I returned to Tasmania in the interests of regaining what after all are roots deeper than even my European ones.

My story of restlessness arising to a large extent out of a search for my 'true home', with its attendant sense of dislocation and disorientation is to be found in my seven books of poetry: *Remote Corners* (Twelvetree Press); *In The Shadow of Van Diemen's Land* (Cornford Press); *Life Given* (Ginninderra Press); *A Tasmanian Paradise Lost* (Walleah Press); *A Post-Colonial Boy* (Fullers); *At Large* (Ginninderra Press); and An *Inherited Epic of Gilgamesh* (Ginninderra Press).

An eighth collection, *Another Love, Another Life*, is soon to be sent forth in quest of publication, and I am currently at work on a prospective ninth entitled *A Tasmanian Tale*.

ALLAN JAMIESON

Allan Jamieson retired in 1999 after a long working life as a chemical engineer in the pulp and paper industry, living on four continents and visiting 21 countries for business purposes. He has resided in Burnie since 1981.

He began writing books in the early 2000's. So far, he has published seven non-fiction books and one compendium of short stories (*Meandering Mind*). The non-fiction titles for which copies remain for purchase are:

- *Voyage through the "Big Empty"* (container ship passenger from Melbourne to Philadelphia)
- *Honto Henro* (the 88 Temple Buddhist Pilgrimage in Japan)
- *Service Above Self* (75-year History of Burnie Rotary Club 1942—2017)

- *Enthusiastic Amateurs* (a cautionary tale for golf and sporting clubs)
- *No Return* (life of Rachel Newton 1803-1855)

For more information, see <https://fawwritersnorthwesttasmania. blogspot.com/>
For copies of Allan's books, email Allan at aoki@southcom.com.au

In late 2016, Allan decided to write his first novel and he is now in search of a publisher for this book.

MEG McLAREN

Meg was born on the island of Trinidad, in the West Indies. She had a happy and colourful childhood and her writing is influenced by these experiences. Over the years she has travelled extensively and has come into contact with many different lifestyles. She is now retired and lives in Tasmania where she is able to pursue her love of writing.

DAWN MEREDITH

Dawn has a head full of dragons and robots, but somehow managed to teach children with learning disabilities for 28 years, rather successfully. She has always been a book worm, annoying her family while growing up and now as a mum, she has passed on that habit to her daughter. Dawn moved with her family to North West Tasmania in 2018 where she has a gorgeous little studio facing valleys and mountains, the perfect setting for flights of fantasy. She absolutely adores gardening. Dawn is keen to try archery and blacksmithing. She has a Fine Arts degree & speaks fluent Norwegian.

Dawn's first book with Shooting Star, *Flight Book 1 – Rebel*, will be published in late 2019. Rebel tells the story of a young rebel called upon to lead… with a broken wing and absolutely no idea what he is doing.

KIM PEART

Born in 1952, Kim was raised by the Derwent River in Howrah, as the old farmlands were being transformed into a modern suburb.

Kim studied art in Hobart, launched a Viking society in Tasmania in 1975, and engaged with space settlement visions in 1976.

Pursuing space related ideas, Kim engaged in Second Life in 2007, a virtual world where the user creates the content, and discovered a global creative community in an environment build on art.

In 2018 Kim conceived of a writing technique using Second Life, by focusing with his avatar to write poems, and later a short story.

Kim has researched many topics over the years, and written innumerable articles, as well as writing the occasional poem.

The technique of focusing on the writing of a poem via his

avatar has delivered surprising results, with 38 poems composed in ten months.

Each new poem is put in a Notecard in an illustrated board in his Poems Galley in Second Life.

Kim is about to set a selection of the poems out on a poetry trail in Ross, where he now lives, and works on a book on space and human futures.

LESLEY PODMORE

Lesley lives in the beautiful fishing village of Stanley on Tasmania's far north-west coast, with its magnificent beaches and inlets, and the iconic Uluru-like volcanic remnant, the Stanley Nut.

Her newly acquired interest in serious writing has only come to the fore in the last ten years. She writes poetry, and is currently working on a series of books for young children.

Lesley was born in Smithton 70 odd years ago, where she was educated, and then re-located to attend the University of Tasmania in Hobart.

She taught primary school, (prep, and grades 1 and 2) in various locations around the world from 1962 to 1973, until marrying and beginning her life as a mother in Brisbane.

She belonged to the Nursing Mother's Association, and gave introductory talks on breast feeding to expectant mothers. She also became an active member of the Queensland Playgroup Association while the children were small, and for a year took on running the playgroup's toy lending library for groups south of the river.

Her father had a natural talent for poetry, and the family background gave her a good grounding in music, painting and acting. The family had a thriving veggie patch. Veggie growing became the norm for her where-ever she was living, and this led to an interest in nutrition when the children were small. She enrolled in naturopathic college and went on to gain qualifications in nutrition and kinesiology.

Lesley brought her family to live in Tasmania at the end of 1986, where they settled in the hills behind Somerset. She learned tai chi and then went on to teach Adult Ed. classes in tai chi and a number of allied health related topics, and is currently running classes in Mindfulness.

As well as writing, Lesley practises yoga, plays harp with Harpeggio, (a Burnie based ensemble), and paints in watercolour and pastel. She also volunteers with Landcare, and BirdLife Australia in their current shorebird monitoring project.

BRENDA SLAVOFF

Brenda has written poetry, plays, short stories and novels. Many of them were based on the author's vivid dreams. One of her novels has been read in serial form on radio, two of her plays have been performed and she has published many short stories and poems - and all this between gardening, theatre, composing music, playing the harp and dancing the tango.

LILLIA WILLIAMS

My parents were both born in Poland; during the war my dad was in Auschwitz and my mother was raised in an orphanage and then worked on a farm as a farm hand.

Once they immigrated to Australia they started a family. I am one of 5 children 4 girls and 1 boy. I was born in 1954 in a town called Penrith in New South Wales.

At home Polish was the only spoken language and I could not speak English until I went to kindergarten. After leaving school I worked at many office jobs and then qualified as a purchasing officer at Westinghouse Brake and Signal Division.

In 2004 I did an interior design and colour course, then a writing course a jewellery course and a cooking course.

After a short visit to Tasmania in 2007 I decided to move here in 2012.

Then in 2016 I met Stephen and we married and moved to the farm at Boat Harbour –Heavenly Farm – and we are retired from working life.

We have surrounded ourselves, with many animals; sheep, cats, peacocks, turkeys, chickens, goats, alpacas, dog, fish, sea horses, cannery…

www.ingramcontent.com/pod-product-compliance
Lightning Source LLC
Chambersburg PA
CBHW071108100726

47908CB00008B/2311